QUEENS OF DELIRIA

Michael Butterworth
based on an idea by Michael Moorcock

Collector's Guide Publishing Inc

To Mike, Elric and Jerry – with thanks

Copyright © 1977, 1995 Michael Butterworth

All rights reserved. No part of this book may be reproduced or transmitted in any form or by any means, electronic or mechanical, including photocopying, recording, or by any information storage and retrieval system, without permission in writing by the publisher.

Published by Collector's Guide Publishing, Box 62034, Burlington, Ontario, Canada, L7R 4K2
Editor – Carl Krach

Manufactured in Canada
Queens of Deliria / Michael Butterworth
ISBN 1-896522-07-6

HAWKCRAFT INVENTORY

BARON BROCK - (David Brock) lead guitar, 12-string guitar, synthesizer, organ, and vocals

THE THUNDER RIDER - (Nik Turner) sax, oboe, flute and vocals

LORD RUDOLPH THE BLACK - (Paul Rudolph) bass and guitars

THE HOUND MASTER - (Simon King) drums and percussion

ASTRAL AL - (Alan Powell) drums and percussion

THE SONIC PRINCE - (Simon House) keyboards, mellotron and violin

CAPTAIN CALVERT - (Bob Calvert) poetry and vocals

THE CRYSTAL PRINCESS - (Rickie) dance

THE LIGHT LORD - (Liquid Len, Jonathan Smeeton) lights

Parliament Hill was all that remained of the once proud and noble city called London.

It was all that remained of any part of the cities and conurbations and other human artefacts that had once existed on Earth; for little had been able to survive the fighting and rioting that had characterized mankind's selfishness and greed. Little, that is, save for 500 screaming, cheering individuals who were gathered at the summit of the hill. They were the descendants of the survivors of the holocaust who had first gathered to listen to the final, great rock concert held in the ruins after the wars had wreaked their worst.

The concert had lasted many months and out of it a new society had been formed, based around the ideas of the young, the aware and the Hawkwind sounds. Refugees from all over Earth had been attracted by the music, limping in as best as they could on the remains of technology and the energy of sheer determination. But as they fashioned their new lives, disaster struck again.

The forces responsible for mankind's downfall, not content with their crushing victory, had wanted complete power over Earth. They had manifested themselves in the form of human agents and a long and trying battle between Hawkwind and the Dark Forces had commenced. At the outcome, the concert city had been demolished. Earth herself had almost been shattered into dust. A pocket of survivors, including Hawkwind, had remained. But weak and few though they were, they had triumphed. The Dark Forces had been banished and peace had reigned for a hundred and fifty years. This century and a half later, the night was alive with sound and colour again. The Children of The Sun had grown once more in numbers and had come up from their new homes on the plain beneath the hill to the sacred concert site where, each year, Hawkwind gigged in celebration of their former victory.

They yelled with madness, and they had every right to be insane. For now, after a hundred and fifty years of peaceful development, the same Dark Forces were returning.

The children were angry and frightened and already suffering from the crippling symptoms of the Death Rays. While the Hawkwind music played, they were safe. They were protected by the unique, healing power of the space music and the band of immortal Superlords who produced it.

In the centre of the crowd's dark midst, illuminated by the orange lights of the fires, the coloured twinkling lanterns and the bright stage lights, the Spacecraft played.

Its engines thudded wildly.

The deadly, sonic sounds whined and careened through the air, calling out to the last pocket of life on the besieged planet, beckoning them towards it.

The violet coloured searchlights probed majestically, relentlessly over its massive engines. They beamed out an SOS to whoever or whatever could see them.

All remaining life on Earth was needed to participate in the coming battle if the Dark Forces were to be overthrown once and for all.

BOOK ONE

LAND OF THE SUPERSTARS

DARK ANGEL

The Hound Master, legendary Tamer of Beasts, rode in on his great black winged *capriccio* from Hell.

He flew impetuously across the darkened landscapes of Earth towards the distant lights of the Hawkwind stage.

Already the night air was charged with the strident, negative energy of the Death Rays and his long golden hair streamed from his head as he raced harder against the wind.

His imperious lips parted with a snarled excitement and he threw back his head and laughed at the Death sparks which flashed around him.

And as he flew, his mind burned with a thousand random thoughts.

Until now, he had shunned the company of his fellow Lords and mortals in a relentless search for the sacred Life Sword — the libidinal, regenerative font of power that legend told would be found amongst the debris of civilization. It was a sword fashioned from matter so rare and ethereal that no mortal or even ordinary immortal could hope to wield it. Only when the favoured hero gripped its elusive shaft would its billions of atoms solidify into a firm and erect mass. In that hero's possession, a pathway to Earth's centre could be cut to where the Death Generator, controller of the Dark Forces, lay entombed. Such a hero would be able to cut the cancer directly from Earth's heart and free humanity forever from its bondage.

But the Hawklord had roamed in vain. He had searched for the Life Sword's whereabouts, and still the Death Generator cast its malevolent influence across a world in pain.

Time had outwitted him.

After a hundred and fifty years, the Era of Peace — the First Era of the Dawn Age which had succeeded civilization — was being vanquished.

"Hell Hound! Faster! The puny strength of the Dark Lords try their luck against us once more! I must get to my drums so I can show them who the real Lord is!"

He let go of the reins to give the creature its maximum lee.

Its straining muscles buckled beneath his command as its wings beat faster and more heavily against the tortured air.

Below them, the agonized land, still scarred and as yet unreclaimed, fled fearfully from them as they drew closer to their destination.

THE PSYCHEDELIC WARLORDS

A lone, fuzz guitar howled in the night.

It was a prolonged, insistent growl of electrified steel that won the approval of the screaming crowd which had crushed itself against the stage.

The stage shook and shone, a great living eye of colour and light and sound in the primitive darkness, its surface like a huge target board agleam with curving rainbow bands of red, green, blue and gold. Buttress-like piers supported the two drum kits as well as the four squat assemblies of the searchlights that beamed up their violet-hued rays into the sepulchral clouds, while at the centre where the bulls-eye would have been, on a wild, painted backdrop of stars, lay the unique machines and controls of the Hawkwind Spacecraft.

While the ominous, introductory note to *Reefer Madness* began, the Thunder Rider, War Lord of The Sax Horn, lowered his trusty Selmer Mark 6 from his lips. He paused, waiting for the note to fade away.

Gradually, from the depths of the Spacecraft there came another sound — a rising, rumbling tide of rock music. Long menacing notes and drum rolls burst out from the giant speaker cabinets. They circled around the back of the cheering Children — and with a roar, the thunderous body of the number broke out.

The hardware howled, straining at its electronic hatchways. Lights flared and melted madly around it, and when the crescendo of sound had reached its peak, then the Sax Lord put the sacred reed back where it belonged.

He blew all along the huge perimeter of the circular stage, his jacket of crimson and gold streamers and his wild red hair flaring out behind him like the rockets of his own propulser pack.

Then tall, laconic Lord Rudolph The Black swung his shining black Gibson *Boneshiverer* from his hip. Drawing the notes from his instrument with strong, sure fingers, he laughed darkly into the night. So permanent a fixture was his famous, mysterious smile that it seemed to almost detach itself from his face and hover above the crowd. His devil's wet-look suit and flowing black cape glistened, and his illuminated bow tie flashed cryptically. Like his smile he had come mysteriously one night, crashing through the planes of Time from the Pre-Dawn Age. No one knew from where or by what forces he was conveyed, but everyone was glad that he had made it. The War Lord played on, gleaming and glowing, flashing and smiling, enjoying whatever Fate dealt him.

Behind him stood Baron Brock, cheerful Keeper of The Machines, taking the lead on his killer guitar, *Godblaster*. Disposed to the most fitful moods of anger, he was now paradoxically cheerful, as though he enjoyed nothing more than to play to humanity on such a grim occasion as this. The clean, dead landscapes of Earth seemed to excite him. The prospect of danger brought him to life and he moved powerfully though composedly about the stage. His long fair mane flowed luxuriously down his old suede cowboy jacket. He was careful enough though, to hang back against the motionless banks of the amplifiers and synthesizers that formed the central octogonal hub of the Spacecraft. From time to time he made adjustments to the controls, modifying and changing the awe-inspiring sounds.

At the far corners of the stage, where the massive searchlight assemblies were mounted, each with their own silhouetted controller, crouched the two large drum kits — one on each trembling pier. They were the two engines of the Spacecraft, endlessly thudding and reverberating. But only one of the them was manned. The other seat lay empty, waiting for the roaming, questing Master of The Hounds to return from his adventures and take its controls. In the meantime, Astral Al, alias Powell The Power, alias Supreme Lord of Chaos, kept the vital forces flowing, hitting his Ludwig drums like an animated stone colossus.

The Sonic Prince, caught in a bright spray of crimson light from the projectors, delivered a volley of scales from his electric violin, the like of which no man had heard since Joshua had brought down the walls of Jericho more than twenty centuries before. Each volley was wilder and more demonic than the last. He leaped madly, swaying toward the crowd at the edge of the stage, his brow furrowed by intense concentration as he stabbed and scraped his metal bow across the strings.

The Crystal Princess, The Queen of Acid Rock, jerked and shook her large Amazonian frame beneath the strobe lights, interpreting the music with a wild and savage eroticism.

Liquid Len, The Light Lord, and the many ranks of the Light that he commanded sat vigilantly at their posts directing the consoles of the giant projection towers that blazed their exotic colours and dreams on the band.

And, no less a Lord of War for all the finery and singularity of his dress, Captain Robert Calvert stood on the flashing panels of the Hawkwind Star Ship. He struck an awesome pose, garbed in the boots, flying jacket and goggled headgear of a fighter Pilot from the First World War. He wore a pair of thick tweed riding-breeches, and at his hip rested a Tommy gun and a space magazine clip. Yet he had no real need for the crude military trappings he sported. Round his throat he wore a lilac scarf, flamboyantly knotted, and in his hands he held only a sheaf of poetry and an electric megaphone. His goggles were pushed back over the antique casque, revealing pale, Bryonic features that gazed dreamily over the bobbing heads of the Children. With strong voice he sang the words of the number through the megaphone. The result proved that if mankind had once been in need of the mechanical weaponry of war, now it had no further use for it.

The Hawkwind music was a love and a weapon of its own.

It was a rich and blissful sound.

It was an urgent, compelling sound, almost desperate in the insane manner of its generation. The crazed crowd raised their hands above their heads in despair and anguish, pleading for an even higher volume, for an ever greater intensity of the musical experience.

The Children of The Sun craved for something which no band could give them to the full, except in death. For they had become motivated by more than the pleasure of merely listening to music. A sinister, urgent need was detectable inside them — a need which matched the voracious force of the music. It was as though rock band and fans were locking in an eternal, evil embrace, each needing the other and never getting their due satisfaction...

WINDS OF TIME

Shrieking and sighing through the desert airs the ghost bodies of prisoner astronauts lived.

They flitted coldly about, rootless, never able to rest or die. They lived their vaporous lives in perpetual torment, bemoaning the theft of their flesh.

The wild, exhilarating music of the Hawklords reached them halfway round the globe, where they drifted. Their soundless voices screamed out, enraged by the picture of love and life which the music evoked.

"Mistress Queen!" they implored the Invisible Red One who controlled them. "Over the timeless generations that have been ours we have at last managed to track down the Hawklords as you wished. They stole our bodies and gave us poison! They killed off our loved ones and brought down our houses and brought our Mother Earth to this! Thanks to them we'll never drink our beer again or lay our loved ones! But now you in Your Magnificence have give us the chance we need to live again! Thanks to you, Invisible Red One..."

Their voices trailed away, half-heard, half-understood.

Once, their ghostly flesh had taken real form and shape. Criminals from the Pre-Dawn Age and veterans of overloaded jails, they had been jettisoned into space, several hundred strong, locked away from the computerized engine rooms that were timed to drive their ships away for the duration of their sentence. But by the time that their sentence had expired, Earth had died. The land they knew had gone. The friends they had were dead.

They had returned to find that their sentence had only just begun…

DOCTORS OF MADNESS

Deep in the subterranean laboratories beneath the wide sighing deserts, the Earth Scientists felt the plaintive call clutch and tug at their anaemic skins. Ever since the great Earth ships had left the Mars colonies and their ancestors had travelled back home across the gulf of interstellar space to a ravaged Earth, they had buried themselves away from the world and the past. They had dedicatedly researched for strains of plant life able to take root on the barren soils above and cloak Earth once again in its green mantle. They knew that soon, without plant growth, the atmosphere would become poisoned with lethal carbon gasses.

Apart from the Hawklords, the Children of The Sun, the ghosts of the prisoner astronauts, and one other, lonely man, the Earth Scientists were all who remained alive.

The powerful waves from the Delatrons undulated across the lifeless sands toward them. It reached inside their minds and bodies, and they knew that now there had been another setback in their plans. Once a year for the last hundred and fifty years they and their ancestors had felt the music's glorious effects. Once a year they had even ventured to travel to the site of the stage, to their allies, the noble Hawklords. The effects had been peaceful and calm, but now they detected a note of desperation and anger. They knew that the callers — that all Earth — badly needed their help.

As one they put down their test tubes and turned off their instruments.

They picked up their deadly electronic weapons and began climbing into the white rays of the sunlight…

ACROSS THE WOUNDED GALAXIES

Tall, morose, Elric of Melniboné heard the Hawklords' call. He stood alone on the cracked and dying Earth, the Wind of Ages blowing through his aching heart. He looked painfully about him, straining to see in the bright lights of the new world.

The emanations seemed to come from the horizon where the endless rocky escarpment fell. They pulsated wondrously, melting his dreary being and filling it with hope of fresh life. It was a music he couldn't hear, only feel. It was a cryptic code that only his body knew how to decipher.

Puzzled but pleased, he started out across the rocks towards the source of the sound. It was the first sign he had in this barren world that there was anything in it but the elemental components. As he journeyed, a deeper, darker part of him still shuddered with the despair and the knowledge of death. He had been flung from an earlier, richer land. Condemned once already, in his own time, to wander an Earth which hated and feared him, now he was faced with an even greater vengeance at the hands of fate.

In his anguish he brooded deeply.

Once he had belonged to the proud and noble land of Melniboné, which for a hundred centuries had ruled Earth. Then its line of kings came to an end and he, Elric, last son of the last king, had been forced to wander a changed land which had ostracized him. With his Hell Blade, *Stormbringer*, a sword composed of the substance of Chaos, a ravisher and destroyer that drank the souls of its victims he fought against his enemies and defeated them. The detestable wilderness of anarchy had been brought to an end. But then, there had been no place for the Hell Blade. Frustrated by the conflicting forces it served, it had gone toward the side of Chaos, its natural bent, and it had slain the man who bore it.

Even after death, Elric's wandering and restless soul had gained no comfort. He had been brought through into the desert world that now surrounded him — a world more alien to him than the other, a world in which he had no place at all.

Stormbringer had returned. It hung in his scabbard at his side. Savagely, he cursed it. He remembered when it had dipped into his own royal blood. It had given him a bitter pleasure. In death, at least, he had expected the life of a transient spirit. Tormented, yes, but free of his accursed physical flesh. At the most he had expected merciful oblivion. Instead he had been born healed, on yet another lonely and despising plane.

Angrily, he looked behind him at the bank of grey mist that rolled away along the horizon. Out of that he had been reborn. But the land of his rebirth was even more inhospitable.

It stretched away on all side, a featureless slab of cracked and deadened rock.

There was no rest for his aching heart...

GREY, FLICKERING FRAGMENTS OF THE FUTURE

The dealer dealt another set in the endless game of cards he had devised for himself.

His hand skimmed the green felt surface of the small card table he had erected.

Thoughtfully, he studied the array of faces and symbols. From a second pack he dealt a fresh hand. He compared the two sets.

All around him were the wild sounds and flashing lights of the Spacecraft. The air was smoky with the hundred fires that burned, providing the Children with heat and hot food.

As he played, ideas sprang into his mind. They were produced partly by reasoning and partly by the patterns followed by the cards themselves. His mind fed skillfully off the possibilities opened by the game of chance.

With the cards he could foretell fragments of the future.

As he dealt he watched the band performing. They were his boys. He had managed and moulded them. Back when it mattered he had booked them in at the best gigs…when there had been gigs to do and people to gig to and places to gig in. He had dealt them his best hand. Since then, the world had gone mad. The old order had gone. There was nothing left for a manager to do; so he just sat about quietly, dealing, reading the future for his boys.

He smiled. It was the self-satisfied knowing smile earned from hard years of experience in the business.

He was small of stature but well-built. He had on a straight, grey suit. When the boys first saw him they though he was a Straight., but he quickly proved them wrong.

As the music thudded and crashed all round, the smile left him abruptly.

He stared down disbelievingly at the upturned faces of the cards.

So the boys were right. But they were wrong, too. The future was bad, sure…but it was worse than even they suspected.

Scratching his neck he leant back in his chair and pursed his lips. Out of habit he reached for the cigar in his mouth, but it wasn't there. He pulled his arm away, annoyed.

He hadn't had a cigar for one hundred and fifty years…

THE BOSS MAN'S LAST STAND

Finally, the Boss heard the sound of Hawkwind.

The music pierced through his crazed sleep as he rested up in the purpose-built Time Vault at the side of the stage.

It pounded fiercely, battering the walls of the tough building. In here, the band's equipment and stage clothing was stored, kept safe from the deteriorating effects of Time. The doors were timed to open with the yearly gigs and then close again, but to cope with the present emergency they had been forced open prematurely.

His heavy jowls trembled as the serene notes pierced in and out of his dreams. He snored fitfully, oblivious to the desperate changing of powers outside. Right now he was not needed, but when his charges at last came off the stage, then he, the Boss, would have to wake. The job of clearing off the equipment and putting it back into its store would begin.

The Chief Roadie turned in his sleep. He was another whose true role had largely ceased to exist when the old order had collapsed.

He was completely crashed out, lying half on and half off a large colourful cushion. Suddenly the beautiful sounds that complemented his dreams stopped.

The buffeting stopped.

The pleasure drained away. In its place came the cold, nauseating grip of the Death Ray, now uncombatted and free to do its worst.

He woke immediately, his eyes wide and bloodshot. A sickly feeling had built up inside him. His skin crawled with invisible insects that seemed to burrow beneath it. He turned quite cold.

Part mortal, and only part Hawklord, he was vulnerable to the effects of the Death Rays.

With a look of displeasure on his face, he climbed groggily to his feet and staggered away...

A smacking, flapping sound of great wings beat at the air.

The Hound Master's *capriccio* appeared, caught in the violet beams of the searchlights.

With wings raised high above its head and talons outstretched, it began dropping down the pillars of light toward the stage.

But it had arrived too late for its rider to partake of his drums. The other figures on the stage had stopped playing and they were making their way offstage accompanied by the agonized shouts and screams of the Children.

Impatiently the Hawk drummer jumped down from the creature's back as it landed, and he ran after them.

MUSIC OF DEATH

In the pitch darkness of the small closet the Boss sat weeping and cursing. Several minutes had elapsed since the thunderous music had stopped playing and there was no sign of it starting again.

He shuddered in the grip of the negative force. In the absence of the protective music it was a thousand times worse than usual. The minutes seemed like hours of agony to his sensitized abdominal system, and he rued the day he had been spirited off from his cosy rooms in long ago Notting Hill. Until recently, Chief Roadie Higgy had presided over the affairs of the band. But the time had come for the faithful Scot to depart. The Godly powers that seemed to guide the new Earth had decreed, for reasons unknown to anyone, that certain numbers of the band had to be returned to their former equilibrium and others brought to replace them. Where they were taken to, no one knew — perhaps back into the old Pre-Dawn Age, or to some other place where their brand of artistic weaponry was needed to fight off the Dark Forces. Lemmy, the infamous Count Motorhead, had been amongst those who had been called. So had Stacia, dancer extraordinaire, Actonium Doug and Higgy. But the Boss certainly remembered where he had been brought from, and wished with all his heart that the Gods had never thought of standing him in the old Scotsman's boots.

His stomach heaved as another wave of Dark buffeted nauseously against him and the blackness spun violently around.

He clasped his head and groaned. Out of all the people in Earth City he had to be the only one affected in this way. Most of the people simply had the Horrors…they had pains and nightmares, and their bodies stang. Bad enough. But he had to have the sickness as well, and there was nothing he detested more.

The Rays that caused the symptoms had been unknown to man until Hot Plate and the Sonic Prince had discovered them long ago while working in the Buckingham Palace laboratory. No one knew quite what their insidious composition was, but they knew its effects. For some reason, the Cyndaim Wave Radiation, as it had been technically described, was unable to pass through the partial vacuums of outer space. Contrary to all scientific laws known to mankind, empty space actually reflected them. Once generated, the waves could not escape. During the wakeful eras of the Death Generator, therefore, they gradually built up in the atmosphere.

For centuries the Death Generator had slumbered at the heart of the planet, keeping all of humanity under its control. It had been placed there millennia ago by two warring alien races — remote antecedents of mankind called the Basaak and the Throdmyke. Occasionally it had awakened and plunged Earth into successive Magic Ages. Two Magic Ages had been recorded by men, and each time its power had been forced to decline by older manifestations of the Hawklords. On the third occasion, the last, mankind had been all but destroyed.

For the whole of their existence men had been oblivious of the cause of their misery. The sleeping dragon at Earth's core had eventually been discovered by Hawkwind — by accident. The Sonic Prince and Del Detmar, former electronics genius with the band, had invented a musical processor called a Delatron. Their aim, and its purpose, had been to modify and enrich Hawkwind's music, but inadvertently, the new kind of music it produced had somehow awoken the Death generator.

With the aid of their ill-fated scientist friend, Hot Plate, they had been able to pin-point the location of the satanic machine. But, in its impregnable position, the Death Generator was an impossible enemy to defeat. By building more Delatrons and incorporating them into their musical equipment, they had only been able to destroy its human manifestations.

Mysteriously, the Death Generator's powers had subsided and had returned to rest of their own accord.

Now, they were awakening again. Perhaps it was the Hawkwind music that had triggered them off, perhaps the unknown timings in the Generator's heart.

The Boss writhed around in agony in the closet, clutching at his stomach as bitter thoughts surfaced inside his mind.

He bellowed out in sudden rage, making a futile attempt to fight off the invisible forces that bent the darkness and sprang at his body. He would have been better able to withstand the effects of the Death Rays if that had been all he had to contend with. But recent events had suggested that once again the Death Generator had found an agent through which to operate. Not merely an immobile, perhaps lifeless, piece of machinery like itself but an agent that was able to move around on the surface of the planet ensuring that its work was done properly.

Evocative pictures flashed through his mind and he tried to dispel them. These pictures were the real reason for Earth City's wrath. They were the real reason for the tumultuous rock music that had been played. The reason why the Hawklords had decided to finish off the Death Generator for good.

The mental pictures clarified, and he groaned again.

Mounted on their Starstreakers — single-seated machines that flew through the air — had been the proud and noble, though fatally innocent children of the Hawklords. One was Patti L'Horse, the pale beautiful daughter of Thunder Rider; the other was Lord Jefferson of Polyddor — the tall, striking son of Lord Rudolph The Black. With them were the other members of Patti's band, a unique and virile ensemble of hand-picked musicians known as The Complete Orgasm Band. They had all been mounted on their machines, instruments on their backs, and Starstreaking off into the distance. They had left with the intention of founding a new frontier City beyond the Westlands. And that memory of them, of *her*, was last occasion they had been seen. They had disappeared months ago, seemingly off the face of the Earth. Contact with them had ceased. A search party had failed to find them. The looming threat of the Death Rays that coincided with their disappearance suggested that treachery rather than accident had been to blame — and the Hawklords were too familiar with the methods employed by Death Agents to subvert and terrorize their victims to think otherwise.

Now the physical pain and sickness seemed to fade into the background, and the far more terrible pain of grief began to tear at the Boss's mind. He cried out in the darkness. He hauled himself from the closet and crashed out through the door into the Time Vault's changing area. He had hoped to blot out the images of Patti, but he realized now that it was useless. The picture of his lover would never go away until he had travelled space and time and endured a lifetime of misery to find her and bring her back.

In front of him the door leading to the stage burst open and the fiery figure of Thunder Rider entered.

THE AUBERGINE THAT ATE RANGOON

Thunder Rider paused for a moment before entering, sensing that the Boss was unwell. He strode into the small room, shaking his head grimly. Rings flashed on his fingers and in his ears. His long, red hair swung round and the coloured streamers adorning his cloak spun out as he turned to face the members of the band entering the room behind. It took a great deal to rouse a normally easy-going person like him to such a pitch of anger.

"We'll have to take action…I can't bear thinking about her," he cried.

The others threw themselves down on the cushions. They began pulling off their boots.

Astral Al stared at the floor. The Light Lord clenched his arms nervously, pulling off the thick, black jumper he wore.

"What can we do?" he asked, glancing through the open door at the palely dawning sky outside. The massive jewel-like stage was empty now, though still floodlit with the powerful lights. A few Children were staggering about the abandoned controls. Around the stage there was complete silence...except for the cries and moans of pain coming from the stricken Children.

"We should have finished off the Death Generator for good last time it woke," the Hound Master growled. "As we promised to do — and as we were ordained to do."

"We couldn't have kept on playing. We had to stop," the Light Lord continued. He looked distracted. "But we can't just leave everyone to die...unprotected. If we go off in search of Patti and Lord Jefferson what happens to the Children?"

"The Baron's fixing that," Astral Al looked up. "He's organizing the stand-by equipment."

They were reminded of the last time they had used the automatic equipment. Memphis Mephis, one of the Death Generator's agents, had stalked the land. The Hawklords had left the Children protected only by the taped Delatronized music systems devised by Hot Plate and Actonium Doug. In their absence, Mephis and his army of ghouls had broken down the musical defences and almost slaughtered the entire population of Earth City.

"We'll have to make sure that some of us stay behind this time," the Sonic Prince said, stripping off his wide silver trousers.

"I'll not be one of those who does," Lord Rudolph The Black spoke softly. He had been undressing and the smile that usually played on his face was twisted into a parody of its former self. He had lost the zany aura he had given out on stage. He looked at Thunder Rider. "Nor will you, will you?"

Thunder Rider's eyes met his. "No," he said. He flung down his boot in exasperation. His normally happy eyes looked strained.

"I don't see where we can start looking," Captain Calvert said, combing rich revitalized locks in the mirror. He studied himself critically. In the last Magical Era when he had been transported from his luxury London home into the ruins of the future to help fight alongside his crew, his body had been damaged by the pressure of the Old Order as it collapsed. Now he had been fully restored. He looked and felt much younger and his greying hair had returned to its former colour. "There's nothing but a few million square miles of desert and swamp out there..."

"We know they headed off towards the Westlands," the Crystal Princess said. She hung her pink shoulder muffs in her locker, where they would hang until the next time they were needed — probably not for several years, as she did not like to wear the same costume year after year. She gave the Captain a brief, almost sarcastic smile. "We could take the Starstreakers and look for them."

Thunder Rider shook his head. "No we couldn't. We can take the

Starstreakers — but we can't look for Patti in this world. The telepathic contact Lord Rudolph had with Lord Jefferson has gone completely. To all intents and purposes, so has mine with Patti...what I had with her, at any rate. That can only mean that they are either..." he swallowed emotionally, ". . . or they have disappeared into one of the Time Zones. The Captain is right. There are so many Time Zones. It would be impossible to search all of Earth throughout all its ages — for that's what the Time Zones represent."

"Then we can hope," Rickie said firmly. "We can go and search and hope that we find the right Time Zone."

"And how do we know which Time Zone they're in...supposing they are in a Time Zone?" Lord Rudolph asked.

The room fell silent as they thought. The task seemed insurmountable.

The Time Zones had formed after the conflicts with Mephis. Earth, already in ruins, had nearly been shaken to bits with the strain. The power had been so great that faults had occurred in the fabric of Time and parts of the planet had divided into Zones. They were detectable as misty veils of cloud that rose up from the desert floor. Some were thousands of miles long. Other were only patches a few yards in diameter. When they had first appeared, the Hawklords had sent out exploratory parties, and discovered many new and old ages of Earth flourishing side by side. The Local Time Faults were mainly hostile and uninhabitable and Earth City had preferred to stay where it was rather than move into one of them. Then had come the discovery of Matter Compensation. In order to keep stable, the Time Zones had to compensate for material entering them by jettisoning material out into other Times. The reverse was also found to be true. For every venture made into the Zones, part of the matter of that Time Zone was ripped out and flung randomly into the present Time; for each return journey to present Time, an equivalent mass of material was randomly snatched from it by the Time Zone. For the most part, deserts and rocks, people or buildings disappeared, but occasionally the displacement effects were confined to parts of bodies only. This resulted in the most awful maiming. After this grisly discovery, Time Travelling had been forbidden. The Zones had become just another feature of the landscape.

Now, the Hawklords were faced with the prospect of entering into them again and risking the lives of their fellow citizens. Not one Time Zone had to be entered, but many. The search had to be as thorough as possible.

"I think I've got an idea, Lord Rudolph," the Sonic Prince said slowly and thoughtfully. The assembly turned to face him expectantly.

"Patti's Vulvaphone...it's still in storage as you know; she only took her harp with her. Couldn't we take the Vulvaphone with us and use it to help detect her presence?"

Thunder Rider looked up, relieved at the suggestion. The Vulvaphone had been Patti's favourite instrument. He and his daughter had worked on its design together for several years before perfecting it. When they had finished, and she played it for the first time, they had noticed that the instrument continued to respond to her presence after she stopped playing. It didn't seem to make any difference how far away she was from it. It continued to empathize, playing quietly to itself. It had been this instrument, coinciding with the cessation of the telepathic Hawk links between her and her father, that had provided conclusive proof of her disappearance. It had stopped playing.

Thunder Rider laughed. He strode over to the Prince and slapped him on the back. "Of course! That's the answer." He faced the others. "Now all we need to work out is who's coming and who's staying." He looked around questioningly.

The Hawklords had now almost finished changing. Their stage gear, preserved for generations, had been carefully stowed away in the sturdy lockers of the vault. Now they wore strong, cold-restraint garments made by the Earth Scientists from the recycled wastes of the planet. Each had been designed by the Crystal Princess to suit the differing personality needs of the Hawklords who wore them. Basically they were the same; close-fitting jeans, tough boots, sleek warm jackets, Hawk-like helmets and goggles...the latter to protect them from the scathing wind-whipped sands often encountered in the desert.

Astral Al pulled on the tinted goggles and peered through them for a moment. Then he moved the elastic straps upward to the gold wings of his helmet.

"If the Orgasm Band have been spirited away into a Time Zone, we're all going to have to search them out. We need to find and bring them back quickly. It'd be better to leave Earth City unguarded for a short period than to leave it partly guarded for who knows how long. Besides, no one here seems to want to stay behind." He looked around him to test reactions. "I vote we all go."

Thunder Rider looked doubtful, but most of the band seemed to be agreed. "OK," he said. "But we'd better make sure we leave as much equipment running as possible."

As though in agreement, the roaring of the Baron's music equipment began to reverberate against the walls of the Vault. Instantly, the lethal forces of Darkness were pushed back and everyone, particularly the Boss, felt better.

Inside the Vault, the lighting began to flicker and a warning vibration began humming in the air. The timing mechanism of its controls came into operation as the sealing-up process started. Soon, the heavy, protective doors would close on the valuable contents until the next Hawkwind concert was scheduled to take place. Already the roadies were struggling in from the stage with the band's equipment.

"This may be the last time we play," Thunder Rider muttered grimly as he watched, for he had resolved that the coming battle with the Dark Forces would this time have to be a decisive one.

Without waiting for the others he turned and walked out into the chill dawn air.

CANDY FLOSS COWBOY

Through the storage vault doors lay the gleaming stage. It was almost deserted now. Dawn had broken and the huge spotlights had been turned off. Bright wedges of natural light hit the northern cloud masses where the sun rose.

Nowadays the tilt of Earth's rotation was different, and the planet moved more on its axis. Because of this the sun sometimes rose slightly to the west of north, and sometimes it rose slightly to the east. Its rays illuminated the greying colours of the Hawkcraft launch-pad with a cold, supernatural light.

Thunder Rider reached the far side of the stage and dropped down into the open auditorium where the crowds of Children were still gathered, hoping perhaps that a fluke would bring the healing Spacecraft back on its silvery berth. The bright, fiery beacons raised on posts still burned. The camp fires had been left to die unattended.

The Children themselves looked only half happy, uncertain whether the sounds of *Golden Void Part II*, now starting to rumble and whisper from the massive speaker cabinets in front of the stage, would prove to be as effective as the live Hawkwind sound. Some of them came over to talk to the Hawklord, awed by the sight of the winged war-like helmet he wore. He told them of the new plans and they received the news with mixed feelings. A green-haired man stepped forward. A pale, slender woman stood at his side.

"We're behind you, Thunder Rider," the man said. "Patti is our daughter too."

There was an uncomfortable silence.

"But remember," the man continued, "we're mortals. We depend on you. We can't fight off these bad vibes. Without you we're...just nothing."

Thunder Rider swallowed miserably. Together with the Earth Scientists, whom they visited regularly to exchange produce for information, the Children had gradually raised buildings again, tapped underground rivers, grown crops, and started a new technology. It was natural that they should feel anxiety.

The Hawklords themselves would fight to the death for the sake of Earth City, as they had proved in the past.

Thunder Rider shrugged helplessly. "Most of the band feel it's best to make a quick kill. We can't do that if some of us stay behind. But don't worry. We're better protected than we used to be in the days of Mephis. We've had time to get a lot of good equipment together and prepare for a possible attack..." He managed to smile reassuringly, but deep down inside he yearned to be away from the noise and the crowd and the questioning, and steep himself in thoughts of his lost Patti.

He moved away quickly, joining the moving throng that wound its way down the access road from the hilltop to the city below. The roadway was lined with the flaming beacons. Their light shone palely now against the strong light of the dawn, yet their glow still inspired his soul with a feeling of destiny and power. He began to race downhill, his legs streaking out under him. He felt truly immortal in the beacon flames' power, a super-God, running on the energy of the Universe.

Below him lay the low domes of the dwellings and the sprawling construction of the solar energy plants stretching away into the desert. He was soon down among them, treading the black shining streets, running past the lighted windows. Eventually he reached the sacred, temple-like Dome of Machines that housed the weaponry and transportation that the Hawklord would need. Stored here, for safe keeping at Patti's request, was the silent Vulvaphone.

He paused before the smooth plastic walls. Normally the building was kept locked, for few people, in peace time at least, had recourse to enter.

Hesitantly he stretched out his arm and let his jewelled fingers come into contact with the lock. Soundlessly the doors drew back and formed an entrance in the wall. He stepped inside. It was dark, and the lights came on.

It was cold, and warm air began to blow.

But the first thing Thunder Rider became aware of was another presence. Someone had arrived ahead of him.

"Dealer?" he called out softly. He moved forward down a short passageway and came into a large, almost spherical room. Its roof was dome-shaped, with panels that were able to draw back and reveal the sky. In the walls were closed hatches. In the floor, shut recesses. It *was* the Dealer who stood there.

He smiled when Thunder Rider entered. His short, stubby frame was dressed in its usual pin-striped suit. On his head was his fedora, tilted sideways. In the mellow lights of the room he seemed to be the archetypal gangster figure. In his hands, he held a deck of cards.

"I sussed you'd come here," the Dealer said. He looked disgruntled. "How didya know it was me?"

"It wasn't hard to guess," Thunder Rider replied. His eyes glowed with a new power. His skin burned with a far-off intensity. His mind was on distant things, though he felt glad to see their manager. Hawkwind didn't need a "manager" these days, but there were times when cool thinking was a decided advantage. "We need the guns and the Starstreakers. The Vulvaphone...is it still dead?" He moved towards one of the sealed recesses in the floor but the Dealer motioned him back.

"Yeah it's dead. I checked" He paused and wiped his mouth. He felt around inside his waistcoat pocket for a cigar, but remembered there were none. He thrust the thumb of his free hand behind his trouser tops instead. "Listen Thunder Rider. I need to talk to one of you. This mission; it's hotter than you think…"

The Hawklord laughed manically and shook his head, showing off large earrings that flashed briefly. "Anything that comes along, I'll take it. I mean it."

"Then at least listen to what they say. Look…" He held up the cards and showed Thunder Rider their faces. They depicted the royal heads of the Queens — the Hearts, the Clubs, the Spades and the Diamonds. They represented an Age that was long dead and their features suggested a menace which made Thunder Rider shudder. "I've been turning these up all week," the Dealer continued, "and I don't like what they're signifying…Death Generator. It doesn't just come from one place either — that's the strange thing about it. It comes from everywhere. It's a really strong baby…"

"So what do you advise?" Thunder Rider asked. Any advice that the Dealer would give them would be sound and they would have to heed it. He listened intently to the other's reply.

A troubled expression clouded the Dealer's features. He battled silently with his thoughts, then he smiled grimly.

"I'd be the last to try to stop you going…"

Thunder Rider laughed wildly. "I knew you wouldn't say anything else…" He slapped him on the back.

"…but you *must* go adequately prepared, Thunder Rider, and you *must* leave Earth City well guarded!" the Dealer implored him.

"Don't worry," the Hawklord replied. "We've got everything we need in here…"

He looked around the domed room. He strode towards one of the hatches and raised his arm to it. The stones on his fingers sparkled and the door slid smoothly open. His Hawk blood rose in his veins and his heart began to bang violently when his gaze fell upon the wondrous machine inside. He had known what to expect, but the silent presence of the Starstreaker, its silvery metallic beauty and its latent power always thrilled him.

Its parts gleamed and shone. It was shaped like a small seat with a transparent hooded cover and forward-looking visor protecting the seat. On its back was provision for storage. Mounted at the front and sides and on the roof was the machines's formidable array of musical and lighting hardware. Based on the larger prototypes of the Silver Machines built by Captain Calvert years ago at the behest of the Hawk God, these later versions were single-seaters and as a result were more versatile. They flew faster, and could venture where the larger craft could not.

He turned triumphantly to the Dealer. Their manager nodded, grinning himself at the prospect of riding it, although he was not to come along.

Wordlessly, the Hawklord opened the other hatches. Each door slid back to reveal one of the sleek, proud machines. Five of the hatches were empty and he realized with bitterness that these had housed the machines belonging to the missing band.

Eventually ten of the machines lay exposed, ready to ride out on their perilous mission of inquiry, and, if need be, of war.

Thunder Rider stepped back, satisfied. "Now!" he cried. "We'll see if the guns are in such fine condition."

He stooped and with his rings opened one of the recesses in the floor. The panels parted, revealing a storage chamber roughly the size of a man, though deeper. Its walls were lined with small silver packets secured by bands. Gingerly, Thunder Rider knelt down and removed one of them. He unwrapped it and from it took a slim, blunt-nosed, music gun. It wasn't heavy. Its butt fitted snugly into his palm. His fingers easily found the control panel, ready to depress the play button and slide the volume control. Inside the gun's flat, wide body lay the tapes and the miniature amplifiers. In its wide-mouthed nozzle was housed the miniscule Delatron and loudspeakers that would broadcast the Hawkwind sound towards whatever target it was directed.

Experimentally, Thunder Rider switched it on. He was rewarded with a familiar, transistor pitch version of *Kadu Flyer* — one of their later numbers.

"That one seems to work OK," he said. He pulled out a holster and strapped it to his chest inside his jacket. Then he inserted the music gun. "I'll take the first. It might be lucky." When he had finished, he pulled out fifteen other guns and tested them. "Might as well take two of each," he said. He strapped on a second gun and stood up.

"That leaves just one other thing..."

He walked across the Machine Dome's floor until he came to another recess.

"If my memory is correct..."

The door slid open, revealing the exquisite musical instrument. It had been left unpackaged, so that its vibrant strings could continue to play in harmony with its maker, wherever she might be. Its haunting, unearthly sounds had ceased, but *once* they had echoed ethereally throughout the Dome. Its magical voice was silent. Its mechanism stilled.

Tears sprang to the Hawklord's eyes, and he lowered himself once more on bended knee and withdrew the instrument. She had been so beautiful a woman, so perfect a daughter.

Tenderly, he examined the Vulvaphone's strings and the many-headed fret-like vents of the wind pipe that supported them. When the mouthpiece was blown, wind passed through the vents and vibrated the strings — which in turn vibrated a series of paper-thin, bone discs. The strings could then be played like a guitar, but little or no pressure was needed, the fingers merely guiding the sounds which could be amplified electronically.

He put his fingers to the strings, blew down the mouth piece, and began playing. He wasn't very good. The melody he produced was far less even and pure than its fairer operator could have produced, but it was sufficient to prove that it worked. Grief-stricken, he reached down and unplugged the lead from its terminal. He lifted the instrument from its housing and carried it towards his Starstreaker. He strapped it firmly to the back.

All their equipment was working correctly. The arsenal of machinery, refined over generations to perfection, had never been used for war, but now it was ready, perhaps for its first and last battle.

The supernatural forces that had given Thunder Rider and the other Hawklords their powers called out to him now. Their voices called down the centuries, across space and time.

No one knew where the Hawk Gods came from, or why they existed, but each Hawklord knew that he or she had to do their will. They had to rid Earth of the Death Generator and stop the senseless battling of the super war machines.

He felt calmer now. With the moment of their departure at hand, his anxiety left him. He felt sure and confident that they would find Patti. He knew that in some time, in some place, on the desolate mess that Earth had been reduced to, Patti and her band were alive.

Behind him he heard the other Hawklords and lady arriving — Lord Rudolph, The Baron, The Crystal Princess, Astral Al, The Hound Master, The Light Lord and The Sonic Prince — and he motioned them to their machines.

Helmeted and clad in their protective suits and boots they collected their weapons and climbed into the seats. Then the Dome's outer doors flew open, admitting a burst of bright sunlight, and the thought-powered craft began to move slowly along their channels.

They flew towards the clear expanse of blue sky, away from the clamouring, uneasy motions and voices of the city.

CHRONOGLIDE SKYWAY

The ten flying, gliding machines streaked silently, purposefully on their mission of vengeance.

Their simple design gave them the appearance of thrones. They dived and rose in arcs, their hooded roofs and transparent bubble-shaped visors flashing and glinting in the hot sun.

The ten Hawklords inside skimmed across a new Earth; across a land still healing from the scars of ferocious warfare. They sped over its inhospitable terrain, intently watching for signs or features in the landscape that would guide them to their task.

"We must hurry," Lord Rudolph The Black called out in the still, clear air. In his mind hung the image of his son, Lord Jefferson of Polyddor. Like Thunder Rider he had mourned long and hard since the news of his child's disappearance. His normal, easy-going, fun-loving temperament was deceptive; behind the front lay a man of grief and tears. Together with Lord Jefferson he had roamed the planet while his son grew up and reached maturity. For most of the years of peace there had been little to do except map and understand the new conditions. It had been an interesting and absorbing pastime for both.

Earth had been their playground.

Now, all that was in the past. Patti had formed her group, and Lord Jefferson had joined her. As the two had grown older they had spent more of their time away from their parents and often did not return home for months on end. At length they had departed on their ill-fated mission to the Westlands.

As they flew, Lord Rudolph's sorrowful eyes took in the bleak and desolate landscape below.

They had reached the centre of a massive plateau — the remains of a range of mountains once known as the Cambrians, that had stretched down much of the Westlands. It was beyond these, on the shores of the Chemical Sea that the Orgasm Band had set up their base. In these jagged rocks and darkened canyons, plants were beginning to grow again. Dark, fat, hallucinogenic tubers clutched motionlessly at the cracked and ashy surface. Perilous, jagged chasms, their depths in black shadow, rent the crust, in some places deceptive beneath the foliage, in other places gaping hungrily up at them. It was from one such vent that the Hound Master had taken his hell creature. Long ago, colonies of the *capriccios* had been disturbed and overran the deserts, soon to perish horribly from the lack of food. None of the Hawklords, except perhaps the Hound Master, had a natural inclination to linger here, preferring the flatlands of the middle and eastern regions which had been easier to reclaim. But they were impelled by the seriousness of their mission.

"Cheer up, Lord Rudolph," the Crystal Princess called out to him. She had coasted up alongside his Starstreaker and flashed a brief smile across the vacuous rift between them. "I've got the feeling we're going to find them."

"I hope you're right," the Hawklord replied. He beamed at her. "You know, you do good things for me!"

"Look out ahead!" Astral Al yelled.

The drummer's Starstreaker had taken the lead and had been travelling far ahead of the others. Now it returned.

"The first of the Time Zones, they're starting…"

The group became tense. The Time Faults tended to appear in belts along the mysterious lines of force which men had once believed to encircle the planet. The power lines had been linked with flying saucer sightings and other paranormal phenomena. It had been little guessed that they had represented access points into other Time Worlds. It had taken the gross disruptions of the planet's orientation in Time and Space to make this fact clear.

Only a few of the faults nearest to the Westlands where Patti and Lord Jefferson had disappeared had been explored by the Hawklords. The others had been left unentered after the decision had been made to cease exploration.

Each eye looked to the hazy bank of mist on the plateau's horizon.

The bank looked innocent. One could almost fly through it and emerge none the worse for wear, Lord Rudolph thought bemusedly to himself. It reminded him of the layers of photo-chemical smog he had once seen over Los Angeles. But he knew otherwise, and his concern for his son was balanced equally by his concern for those at Earth City. No matter how much he loved Lord Jefferson, if it were not also for the fact that the safety of everyone was at stake, he would not have undertaken the mission.

They sped silently along the plateau towards the silvery-grey Time Fault. As they drew close they could see the breaks in its wall indicating the boundaries of the individual Time Zones. These breaks led deep into the heart of the Fault and to gain entry into the individual Time Zones they had to be navigated.

The bank stretched in a long, straight line, many miles deep around the planet.

When they arrived near to its base, they stopped and gazed at its motionless, almost solid-looking surface.

"How can we possibly search for them all in Time?" the Light Lord asked incredulously.

"Surely the crucial question is, did Patti and her crew enter at this point along the Fault's length?" Lord Rudolph asked. "She might have entered in

Australia for all we know…if Australia still exists."

"We can only hope that they came in somewhere nearby," Thunder Rider replied. "Fortunately the Time Zones themselves aren't all that big. They occupy the same area of space in our timestream as they do in their own. In any case, we've got Patti's Vulvaphone. That should tell us when we enter the right one, without having to search them all."

Astral Al frowned and scratched his head. "Yeah, but I thought the idea of us all coming was to cut down time. How can we when we've only got one Vulvaphone? We could be out there for bloody days!"

"Or years," the Hound Master added gloomily. "But there's no real problem in that sense. My experience of these Zones is that for the most part they're uninhabitable eras. You can tell almost as soon as you've entered which one will support life and which one won't."

"If we each search a Time Zone — that's ten at a time — we can keep a note of the few we come across that might have Patti inside. Then we can go back inside with the Vulvaphone to check."

They kept their formation steady above the baked earth. A cool, welcome breeze sprang up.

"It's going to be a bit bloody hit and miss, isn't it?" the Baron asked after a while.

"What else can we do?" Hound Master asked him.

"We've not got much time for debates," Captain Calvert spoke. He was having difficulty maintaining his height, and seemed to be impatient. Nervous energy leapt off him, causing everyone to feel on edge. "Let's divide up the Zones and get on with it," he added.

"We'll each take a Zone," Thunder Rider said. "If there's no objection?"

There was none.

Lord Rudolph now took the lead and he flew resolutely towards one of the deep, thin vents leading into the bank of the Fault.

INFINITE NEED

The whispering, hating voices of the Prisoner Ghosts bickered and chattered in the desert wind. Their unseen bodies, long ago turned to a fierce energy, moved and spiralled across the Earth, parasitically feeding off all matter in their path.

They occupied any form: tree, house, rock, water or air, that was convenient to their passage. The life patterns were transferred from place to place. The ghosts sped erratically about looking for their victims, mournful and sad, bitter and vengeful.

"Don't underestimate us, Hawklords!" their inaudible voices moaned and whined. "Life was sweet to us! Our memory is long! Now you will give us back our rightful flesh! Don't think you can evade us for long! We will find you, we have all the time in eternity, but *your* time is running out, Hawklords!"

Their envious laughter sounded like a fall of rock in the wind, a whisper in a quiet room, a crash of water in the subterranean rivers below Earth City.

THE UNDYING DEAD

Another figure still struggled across the vast, empty deserts. The misty Time Zone that had spewed him forth lay well behind.

Tall Elric of Meliboné.

He was clad in his armour. The sheath that housed the evil blade Stormbringer swung at his side. Round his neck still hung the Horn of Fate, the godly instrument that had heralded the early days of the decrepit age he now walked in. Had he known what his work would have come to he would never have put the accursed reed to his lips. He would never have sacrificed his trusted friend Moonglum for a world such as this.

He came to a wide pool of dust set in the baked sludge that seemed to constitute most of the desert world. A thin wind blew in the air and whipped its surface. He shuddered as he thought of the fate that would be his if he fell on its surface.

"Hell hole!" he muttered as he traversed its perimeter.

He came to a terrain of hard stones that shone and gleamed in the sun. They were razor sharp and he wondered what force had fashioned them, and now protected them from erosion.

He passed through many different landscapes, all as barren and lifeless as the first, and by the evening, half dead through hunger and thirst, he reached a low range of hills. There he found a raging river that burst briefly through the surface of the earth before disappearing again into the black depths. The waters looked sullen and foul, but he trusted himself to them and drank. He lay down for the night, still sensing the mysterious feeling of pleasure and joy that vibrated in his being. It was weaker now. For a while, out on the desert, the feeling had disappeared, and he had felt more alone and desolate than he had felt in his entire existence. Then it had returned again and kept him going.

As he lay in the cold shadows trying to sleep, he pondered. He had no reason to be in this terminal world, he was sure. He could not feel the presence of the gods here; there was no one to counsel him. It seemed he had been flung here by accident. It seemed he should be dead, after all. Yet if that was the case, what was the meaning of the strange music?

Groaning, he desired that the small, familiar figure of Moonglum, loyal friend and fighting companion of the last of the Melnibonian Princes, would appear from out of the gloom — as his friend had done on many other dangerous missions in the past.

Now that could never be.

An unwelcome darkness fell. The air became suddenly chill. He knew from experience that the cold was not the natural chillness of the night, and he shivered with fear.

A violent pain came in his head and delirious visions formed with frightening rapidity. Pictures of an alien world choked with tall buildings and roadways, coloured speeding chariots that rolled along the thoroughfares, strange twisting faces and figures dressed in unfamiliar fashions, seething crowds and hordes rioting and fighting.

Then voices came, whispering and shouting inside his head.

"All this — once we had all this," the voices proclaimed. 'Elric! Yes, we know your name, and we know where you head. You head towards the enemies who stole our world, and who must be vanquished for their actions. They who heralded the age who destroyed all this, must *die*!"

The voices and the dreams continued throughout the night, and the weakening Prince observed them abjectly and without any resistance or understanding. Eventually, he fell into a turbulent sleep from which he was woken a thousand times.

As dawn broke, his mind cleared and he rose and climbed into the small hills. There, at the end of the range, he came to another of the endless plains that stretched away into the distance. But this time there was a difference.

With bated breath, he noticed a clump of shapes on the skyline. They were buildings, but they were like no other buildings he had seen before. Instinctively, he knew that he had reached sight of his goal. It was from these that the strange musical visions emanated, and he wondered what kind of people or things lived in them.

Between the hills and the distant city lay a severe stretch of terrain that he knew would tax him to his limit, and his weak, albino body was at a desperately low ebb.

From nowhere the voices returned to torment him. They screamed and chattered coldly inside his head. Too weak to fight them off, he could only listen. "There! There! Take us *there*, Elric!" they shrieked. "Take us to the City and we will give you the strength you need!"

A surge of fresh energy came into his being.

Confused and helpless in the grip of the strange world's forces, he set out once more across the inhospitable landscape.

GLOBE OF ANTIQUITY

The narrow fissure in the belt of Time Zones yawned wider as the Hound Master approached it on his Starstreaker. He held on to the safety bar holding him in his seat and manoeuvred his craft between the vaporous walls.

Inside the Time Fault, the air was cool, and seemed to be charged with a strange electric current.

The opaque walls towered above him towards a narrow strip of sky, and fell away to the desert far below.

A narrow path of sand wandered ever deeper into the mass down which he flew.

The walls were semi-translucent and seemed composed of a milky, rubbery substance. The Hawklord knew that they were a gas, albeit no gas before known to man.

He and his machine could move into the Zone with ease.

Somewhere behind him the other Hawklords were entering the belt, at different places, but already thoughts of the world he was about to leave were vanishing from his mind — a common occurrence so close to the energy field which disturbed memory patterns.

He knew that he would have to enter one of the Zones quickly in order to retain his senses. It didn't matter which of the two closest to him he chose. With a deliberate movement he turned and drove himself into one of them.

Immediately his mental grip collapsed and he lost awareness.

He felt his body expand until he had become a being of gigantic proportions, filled with space. Behind him marched a succession of images of himself mounted on the Starstreaker, each figure larger than the last.

In front of him was the grey mistiness stretching on into eternity, although now it was relieved by flashes of colour.

Sounds came and went inside him, crackling and spitting. A pain started at the extremities of his being. Ahead, the future images of himself appeared, each smaller than its predecessor, and he felt himself jumping from one to the other, gradually shrinking until he had returned to his usual size.

A light exploded in front of him and the pain, never intense, subsided.

Gradually, his fragmented senses returned to him.

He had arrived on a deserted cliff-top overlooking a choppy, heavy sea streaked with white crests.

Gulls swooped and circled overhead, crying out harshly.

Below him, breakers crashed on jagged rocks. Behind him, a grassy expanse stretched away towards a thin wooded skyline. The Time Zone boundary was invisible here. The eye was deceived into believing that the landscape stretched further back than it did. But Hound Master knew that it was impossible for any man or thing to walk towards the line of trees without being flung from the Time Zone back into his own Time.

The sea and coastline were deserted, but evidently the Time stream he had entered was life-supportable. Somewhere in it, Patti might be held captive. He could return here again with the Vulvaphone after the Hawklords had regrouped.

He was about to turn and leave the Zone when a series of loud muted reports came from somewhere beyond the curvature of the cliff edge.

Puzzled, he started forward towards them, then remembered that he must not leave the area of land he had arrived on without marking it. It would be fatal to leave without doing so, for in order to guarantee entry back into his own Time Stream, he had to leave this one at the point of entry.

Cautiously, he parked his Starstreaker on the grass and dismounted. He began gathering the limestone rocks that lay embedded in the soft ground and soon had them piled into a mound.

He climbed back into his craft and streaked silently towards the mysterious noises.

The explosions grew louder and more frequent. He approached the edge of the small headland that had obscured his vision, and gasped in surprise.

The cliff edge ran away downhill towards a village. Standing on its brink was a long, straggly crowd of people dressed in strange clothes. Beacons, burning brightly, were positioned at intervals along the edge, surrounded by piles of black brushwood to keep them fuelled. Among the crowd were soldiers armed with primitive rifles, from a period the Hawklord couldn't recognize. But the air was clear and fresh and somehow he knew that the land was England in days when the countryside was still rich and green. It was about midday and the sun was high and warm behind a thin haze of drizzle. The wind was brisk and fresh, and he felt a pang of nostalgia.

His eyes swept out to sea, following the gaze of the crowd.

Not far out lay several fleets of galleys. They were large, proud, double-masted war ships carrying two different insignia. One he quickly recognized as being English. The other ships, perhaps, were Spaniards. Behind the fleets, on the swollen watery horizon, lay a great many other ships, too numerous and too distant to count.

Again the explosions sounded and white puffs of smoke burst along the side of one of the English ships. After a graceful pause, one of the Spaniards returned the cannon fire, sending up fountains of water, short of her target.

Hypnotized and intrigued by the spectacle, the Hound Master pulled down his goggles, drove the Starstreaker off the edge and began flying out towards the ships. A gasp escaped from the lips of the crowd as they spotted him. Soon he was hovering alongside the two great galleys who were exchanging fire. From this distance he could hear the creaking of their rigging and feel the spray of the heaving sea as it lifted off the wooden prows of the vessels. Both ships swarmed with soldier and crew, none of whom had yet noticed the presence of the Hawklord. He manoeuvred himself towards the prow of the English ship. The legendary name *Revenge* was painted gaily on the wood. On closer inspection the other ship proved to be Portuguese, the *Nuestra Señora del Rosario*, though it flew the Spanish flag.

The Hound Master's blood quickened as he realized that he had entered History during the reign of Elizabeth I. Before him was enacted one of the minor battles of Spain's invasion of England. It was the mightiest invasion England had ever faced the Spanish Armada.

Hypnotized, he watched as the *Revenge*, most probably captained by Sir Francis Drake, bore down on the *del Rosario*, her guns blazing. Her opponent returned fire again and began to turn. Then, the entire squadron of Portuguese ships seemed to be thrown into disorder as they struggled to avoid the panicking *del Rosario*. The English ships fell back and kept their distance as the great man of the Portuguese galley collided with one of her own squadron. A loud rending of wood rose on the air, accompanied by shouts and screams from on board. The ship shuddered and both its masts began falling under the impact, crashing down on her decks and scattering everything in their path. For a short while there was silence. Then a detachment of the English fleet, including the *Revenge*, bore down on the stricken squadron once more. They fired their guns and gracefully chased the invaders away toward the vast fleets of the Armada in the distance.

Astounded, the Hawklord ripped his gaze from the scene and turned about.

His being pounded with emotion and tears blurred his vision as he headed back towards the cliff top and departed from the Time of the Tudors and entered into his own, barren, purposeless era.

WHITE PANAMA

A white dot appeared on the horizon.

The whiteness swelled.

It was featureless and try as he might, Captain Calvert could not resolve it with his vision. At first he panicked. He expected, this far through the Zone's wall, to see something more concrete appearing. But this was nothing but whiteness.

He had passed through the Time Zone wall. He had entered a Time perhaps in the future, or the past, where nothing existed. He searched the frightening place of light for life. There was none. Shaking, he withdrew back into the world he knew...

HOT SWAMPS OF LUST

The Sonic Prince stabbed tentatively at the cloud-like wall of another Zone that bulged in front. He had now journeyed deep inside the belt, and he wasn't sure where the others were. So far, he had encountered no habitable worlds. In fact very few of the alternative Times were life-supporting. Mankind had been fortunate to sprout in one that was.

From outside, the worlds all looked alike. It was impossible to tell one from another.

How were they going to remember which ones needed further investigation with the Vulvaphone?

Shrugging, he aimed his Starstreaker at the bulging surface in front of him.

His craft shuddered and he felt his bones being filleted out of his body.

A weird, hazy world began to form in front of his eyes. It cleared, and his bones came back into him again.

He saw a vast swamp filled with rotting frond-like vegetation and brackish pools. Overhead large creatures wheeled. Other living things moved in the water. The air was intensely warm and humid and where the swamps gave way to the sea in the hazy distance, dinosaurs with serpent-like necks played in the shallows.

The shock of being plunged abruptly into a world that *was* habitable paralyzed him with wonder and amazement.

Then he felt a surge of bliss; the swamps activated long-forgotten needs in his body and he found himself longing to swim out towards the dinosaurs. Contrary to all his conditioning, he realized instinctively that dinosaurs were friendly creatures.

But he stopped himself just in time. His feet were sinking in the mud and the remains of his Starstreaker were gradually disappearing. Reluctantly he mustered his thought power into lifting himself out. His craft rose and hovered and then it turned and he phased back through the indifferent walls...

DIALOGUE OF INSANITY

The ground beneath their feet was hard and sandy. The landscape, though flat and almost lifeless, was familiar to them all.

Seven days had passed and during that time they had explored several hundred Time Zones. Only four seemed to be life-supportable. So far, they had tested three of the four with the Vulvaphone, and got negative results. They were waiting impatiently for Thunder Rider to return with news of the fourth. Even as they waited for him to return, they knew their mission had met with failure.

And now also, it had become apparent that their strong, resistant bodies were being eroded by the Death Radiation. The pain of it tingled in their minds and crawled beneath their skins. It had started to affect them only during the last few hours, and they knew if *they* could feel it then the Children must already be near death.

"We'll have to do as we agreed," The Sonic Prince said defeatedly. "Half of us will have to go back and gig; the rest of us stay on and keep searching."

They had dismounted from their Starstreakers and were sitting on the sand. Their helmets and goggles were lying beside them. They were several miles from their first base, deeper into the desert towards the east, and the last thing they wanted to do was call off the search in favour of a gig.

"I don't understand it," the Baron muttered fiercely, almost to himself. "As I remember, Prince, the instruments that you and Hot Plate used to measure the waves showed that they rose in small, steady stages. Last time they took several months to reach this level. This time they've taken hardly more than a week. Either someone is artificially concentrating them like Mephis did with his Death Concentrator, or the Death Generator has stepped up its rate of Cyndaim production. If we knew properly how it worked we would be able to combat it," he said bitterly. "But how can we cut through a planet."

"You're forgetting the Life Sword," Hound Master told him.

"Ah, that's a crazy dream, Hound Master!" the Baron cried hotly. "You keep going on about that, but you've wasted your energy looking for it. It's a dream that will never happen!"

"You're wrong!" Hound Master replied angrily. "The Hawk God told me that the Life Sword was the answer…"

"The Hawk God!" the Baron scoffed. "When did one of them last appear to help *us*? They sit on their thrones and condescend to come down once in every few centuries to see how their experiments are progressing. They're bloody inhuman! They're worse than vivisectionists! When did they supply you with that bit of carrot? I'll tell you when! It was almost a century and a half ago, and they've had you looking ever since! Hound Master, you're crazy! No, the answer doesn't lie in a mythical sword — it lies in our heads, in our arms!" Inspired by his own words he withdrew his music gun and turned it on. 'This is what will fight it!" He looked around him. He leapt to his feet and hauled his Starstreaker upright. Then he pressed the buttons at random on its control bar. Instantly his machine sang with noise. It flashed and spun with coloured, flickering lights.

"You've changed your bloody views!" Hound Master yelled at him above the noise. "You used to think that a bit of agro would sort everything out!" But he remained seated.

Eventually, the Baron turned off his machine and he seated himself. They sat silently for a while, until the Crystal Princess spoke.

"There's no alternative," she said practically. "We must face facts or we're going to waste more time."

"Then who's going to do the honours?" Lord Rudolph asked, smiling distastefully. "It can't be me or Thunder Rider, because we've got vested interests."

An uncomfortable silence fell again.

"It'll have to be those of us who can make up a feasible band," Captain Calvert said eventually. "The Sonic Prince and the Baron, I would have thought, and either Hound Master or Astral Al, myself and the Princess."

"Not me!" Hound Master proclaimed. "I copped for it last time, remember?"

"I'm not going!" Astral Al retorted indignantly.

"Well one of you will have to. We'll toss," Lord Rudolph suggested smugly. He withdrew a long knife from its sheath and showed it to the assembled company. He pointed to his initials scratched in the steel on one side of the shining blade. "See those? They're tails. If they fall up, it means you take up your drumsticks, Hound Master. Heads you do." He indicated Astral Al. With a deft movement Lord Rudolph sent the blade spinning in the air. It glinted, catching the last light of the sinking sun.

It landed in the centre of their circle and they leaned forward to see which side faced uppermost.

"Tough luck, Hound Master!" Lord Rudolph sat upright, still smiling. "It's you."

The drummer grunted non-committally.

The Hawklords who were to return looked disappointed, but they knew that there could be little choice in the matter. Blackest was the Baron. But after his impassioned speech he could hardly try to alter the arrangement.

They sat silently waiting for Thunder Rider to return. They felt the Dark Forces returning to the planet, occupying its deserts and seas once more, trying to claim them for their own.

Soon, the moth-like shape of Thunder Rider's Starstreaker appeared in the dusky sky and landed beside them. He parked his machine and joined them, and they could tell by his silence that the final result on the Vulvaphone had been negative, as they had expected.

Earth was flat…and silent…and endless.

It seemed that despite all their efforts to the contrary, she was resolved to stay that way.

SOUPED-UP LIFE

It was night, the clouds had rolled back and the millions of fierce stars were visible in the darkness. At one time Thunder Rider had lain awake on grassy embankments on cool summer nights, perhaps with a girl by his side, and stared up in wonder at the spectacle. He had dreamed of travelling to distant suns and wondered what the alien worlds that orbited around them were like. Now it seemed as though he really was on one of those worlds. The crazy things that had happened to the band since the days of the grassy embankments were as wild and as strange.

He looked sadly around at the phosphorescent forms of the other three Hawklords beside him. They were not asleep; they *could* not sleep. Each one took the opportunity of night to go into his own thoughts to remember and imagine. Occasionally they lapsed into a kind of slumber, but their immortal bodies needed no charging. Their glowing skins needed no food or sleep and took energy directly from the universal flows that perpetually ebbed around them.

It was strange that they had known both mortal and immortal lives. They had created their band as though from fore-knowledge. As though they had known, all those years ago when the original members had started out in the cellars and clubs of London as Group X, that they would change into beings not far short of gods; battling for the life of mankind. Or rather, fighting for what was left of mankind. Who could even be sure that the preservation of mankind was their ultimate goal? The Hawkwind God had confronted them rarely and then seemingly by chance. He appeared, frustratingly, to have a control over their destiny, and told them only that they must fulfil the Hawkwind Legend and raze the buildings and rebuild the world with parks. The God had not said what kind of creature was to populate such a world. Presumably the Children, but then the Children had been reduced to such slender numbers during the last battle with Mephis, that he was set to wonder.

He groaned aloud.

They had fulfilled part of the requirements of Legend. The last battle had razed everything on the planet! Now it seemed that their final task was impossibly remote. The Children were being cut back yet again. The planet was hopelessly barren.

His reverie was shattered by a sudden visionary glimpse of the suffering left behind at Earth City.

He watched the Children writhing and screaming...

Abruptly, he opened his eyes. Once more the desert appeared before him.

It was cold now; swept with the invisible Death Rays. Somewhere, in some time or place the rays had once again taken over a puppet agent. They were resurrecting another Devil and sending it out towards them on its mission of destruction.

Or were the Hawklords being drawn towards it, dividing their strength and leaving Earth City weakened?

The stars blazed like fires. His vision blurred, and he felt the desert landscape answering him.

Frantically, he tried to fight off the feeling of drowsiness. But the desert faded from his sight and he began to fall, deeper into oblivion.

He came to consciousness in a dark place where there were no stars. A hard, invisible floor supported him in the darkness. It was not warm...or cold. It had no characteristics that he could identify.

For a long moment he remained motionless, wondering what was supposed to happen next.

Then, ahead of him, a door in the blackness opened.

The space behind the door glowed red. He staggered backward and shielded his eyes from the angry brightness of the light.

The red square grew larger.

As it came towards him he could see that it contained hollow spaces where the blackness showed through.

The red and black spaces made a pattern. It was a shape, he realized coldly, a playing card.

The Dealer's muddled predictions came to him.

The Red Queen curtsied, and her face cracked in a smile. She cackled with laughter.

"Come, Hawklord. Your kind are finished...You cannot go back now..."

The metallic red diamonds of her suit danced by the side of her face. He tried to look away from her, but she controlled his gaze.

Slowly, she began to shrink in size. Her laughter faded away and he watched her grow smaller until in his mind she had become no larger than a young girl.

Now, she resembled Patti, fading from sight.

Anxiously he chased after her.

She grew smaller in the darkness and he became frantic that he might lose her. His legs pounded over the invisible floor through the unknown darkness.

But she had gone.

He threw himself down and sobbed.

He cried for a long time, pouring out his grief. Then he lifted his head from his arms as he felt the cold stare of the desert around him. There were stars again.

He arose and shook himself. He looked around for the huddled forms of the other Hawklords, but they had gone.

He started in alarm. Then he realized that it was not they who had moved; it was he. Momentarily his mind had been taken over by a powerful, telepathic hypnosis. The movements he had made in his "dream" had been real.

Half sensing and half dreading what lay behind him, he turned. There, in the darkness lay the cold wall of a Time Zone.

He began to understand. Instinctively, he pulled off the belt that fastened his suit and flung it to the sand to mark the spot where the Zone lay. Then he turned around and began to retrace the steps he presumed he had taken, scarcely able to see them through the tears and the starlight.

FIRES OF NIGHT

In the distant, dark skies, the four returning Hawklords flew. They raced against time to the assistance of Earth City. Behind them the night was illuminated by the ghastly light of an unstable Time Zone. Its pulsations became more frequent and the four fliers hesitated in alarm, wondering whether to return. But they urged themselves on.

Beneath them, large, ominous displacement shapes appeared and reappeared on the desert. The warning pain of the Death Radiation burned more fiercely inside their minds.

The air they passed through had become charged with electricity. Their coldly-glowing Hawk-bodies clashed with the Dark Force's power, emitting blue, crackling sparks.

The horizon ahead of them burst into a lurid crimson glare. The glare lay where the lights of Earth's capital should have been and at first they attributed the excess of light to a freak displacement effect. As they drew close, they saw with horror that it was the light of a fire; not of camp fires or of beacons,

but of several large, roaring, burning masses.
    Earth city was ablaze.

BOOK TWO

THE QUEENS OF DELIRIA

IN THE BLACK SUN

The flickering flames danced brightly from the rooftops of the low survival domes. They seemed almost mischievous, as though, in their antics, they claimed all innocence of how they came to be there. But it was the destruction of Earth City the Hawklords were now watching. They watched with hatred in their hearts for the perpetrators of the havoc.

They were close to the flames and they could feel the heat and hear the crackling as the greedy orange demons ate at the peaceful structures and the gentler technology that had taken so long to build. Above the roaring of the flames rose the sound of the Hawkwind music equipment, pounding out its message of life from the hilltop stage. A riotous mob of people were gathered before the streaming searchlights, madly yelling and screaming. Many had run down along the access road and were pouring through the streets of the city, carrying blazing torches, smashing and firing everything in their path.

The Baron screamed something out, but his voice was lost in the din. He took one further look at the blazing buildings below, then he aimed himself towards them.

His mind powered the Starstreaker like never before and he soon reached the smoke-filled, riot-torn roadways. The crowd was running randomly about with crazed, excited looks on their faces. They carried lengths of piping or any other implement they could get hold of, and were breaking and smashing anything in their way.

Astounded, the Baron realized that these were not invaders — they were the Children.

When they saw the Baron, several of the mob surged towards the spot where he hovered. He stayed his ground, just out of reach of their grasping hands. Wildly he tore off his helmet and goggles to identify himself, and let his long hair stream out.

He withdrew his music gun, and held it aloft.

"WHAT ARE YOU DOING?" he screamed. He stared around him frantically.

His words were scarcely audible above the din. Then he realized that even those who were close enough to hear weren't responding. They had grouped below him, clawing up at him with their weapons, more determined than ever to drag him down.

"VERY WELL THEN, IF THAT'S HOW YOU WANT IT...!" he yelled. He pulled down his music gun and pointed it at them. He pressed the "play" button and the spools began rolling in its snub nose. The music wasn't loud enough to be heard, but a faint beam of positive energy streamed out of its speakers as the Delatronized sound began battling with the negatively-charged air round about.

The other Hawklords had arrived. They hovered beside him, stunned by the nightmarish scene. They pulled out their own guns and desperately sprayed the maddened Children with their lethal rays, but the magical beams had no effect on their targets.

"THEY'RE PART OF US!" the Princess shouted out. "WHATEVER ELSE THEY ARE! WE CAN'T FIGHT THEM LIKE THIS!"

"THEN FIGHT THEM WITH THEIR OWN WEAPONS!" the Baron replied. Grimly he allowed his craft to descend into the hands of the Children. They seemed eager to claim him, as though actually hungry for destruction. But as soon as he felt their first blows, Hawkstrength surged out into his limbs. It arose unbidden, ready to serve in any situation.

Effortlessly he pushed the milling, crushing bodies off, flinging them to the ground.

Kicking and cuffing them aside, he landed his craft and climbed out.

The hordes were upon him instantly, as though they had not yet learned the damage he was causing to their soft bodies. He knew that if he did not stop, the energy inside him would eventually wipe out Earth City. Yet he was forced to fight them.

The entire population was attacking him, shrieking and foaming at the mouths. They came at him with renewed fury and he stared into the eyes of crazed, possessed creatures, and shuddered.

He battered them away from him against the walls of the dome.

Managing to grasp hold of his Starstreaker, he signalled to the other Hawklords for help. They flew over to him in a hail of missiles hurled by the crowd and began holding off his assailants. This allowed him time to climb back into his craft and rise upward to join them.

"GET CLEAR!" he cried out to them.

They hovered in confusion for a moment, then at a signal from Captain Calvert they streaked away from the noise and the flames.

The Baron looked shaken by his experience as they gathered in the fire-light, high above the beleaguered City.

"I can't explain what's happened...I was *killing* them...I've not done that before...It's too weird for me. I'd have killed them all if..."

"You couldn't have done anything else, Baron," the Hound Master said to console him; though his own mind was far too agitated to play nurse. He was desperately trying to think what they could do.

"We've *got* to save Earth City!" he cried out, distressed by the distant sounds of the commotion rising from below. "When I think of all we've done to…"

"Wait!" Captain Calvert shouted. "I've an idea. We could turn off the automatic broadcasting units round the stage — that'd fix them!"

"It's an idea…" the Sonic Prince agreed. "But it's a bit grisly, isn't it? If the full brunt of the Horrors returns to the kids now, most of them will surely die from the strain."

"We've no time to worry about niceties," Hound Master muttered. "It'd be an unforgivable thing to do under normal circumstances, but if we don't do it those "kids" as you call them, will end up burning the place to the ground! Besides, they're in such a bad way that I reckon once they've finished burning things, they'll start on a programme of mass suicide." He shuddered. "Whatever's got into them is far from nice."

"Then let's fly down!" the Captain pressed. "The fire's still spreading. If we stop them now we night we able to save some of the buildings at least."

Against their innermost feelings of concern for the Children, they aimed themselves downward once more.

They set course for Parliament Hill. Its summit soon appeared, illuminated by a mixture of light coming from the Light Lord's equipment (which had been wastefully switched on) and the magical haze of sparks caused by the Hawkwind music as it fought for supremacy with the Dark Forces.

It was taped music, devised by a computerized battery of machines that produced a continuous broadcast. As the five Hawklords streaked earthward, the music machine was playing *The Aubergine That Ate Rangoon*, but as they came in to land on the massive stage, now scarred and dulled, the tracks changed to *Psychedelic Warlords*.

The giant cabinets shuddered and rent the air with the 100,000-watts wall of sound they collectively delivered.

Several hundred Children had gathered. They had wrecked everything apart from the stage equipment. They seemed to be kept from destroying this only by some vestiges of remembrance of their former selves and needs. As soon as they saw the Hawklords they transferred their aggressions to them and swarmed up on to the stage. As before, they tried to pluck the flying craft out of the sky.

This time the Hawklords were prepared. They broke a pathway through the mob and once through, they hovered over the amplifiers while the Hound Master and the Captain landed and began unplugging the cables. The tape decks themselves were in a chamber beneath the stage, but it seemed pointless to waste time with them. In order to save as many lives as possible they had to act rapidly.

One by one, the amplifiers cut out, and the volume of sound decreased. The crowd began to show signs of panic. Already some were in evident pain.

The two saboteurs looked at one another, shocked by the reaction. Grimly, they set about deactivating the last bank of amplifiers. Soon, only one was left working and they cut that out also. The thudding music stopped.

The tortured Children screamed as they received the full brunt of the increased Death Radiation. They shied away from the Hawklords, the invading force inside them now unable to effect its control. In their plight they forgot the Starstreakers, and those that were strong enough ran away aimlessly; the others collapsed and lay dying.

Horrified, the Hawklords finished their grim task, picking up the coils of cable so that they couldn't be re-inserted, and attaching them to their craft.

They rose once more into the acrid air and streaked away toward where they hoped the Dome of Machines, and perhaps sanity, might still lie. The sector of domes on the south side of the hill where the machine house lay was as yet unburnt. They sped rapidly through the roadways, trying to beat the crackling fire which still licked up from the buildings and seemed unstoppable. Uncontrolled fire had not been experienced before in Earth City, except in the days of London when the old City had been razed by the warring fronts of energy in the last magical battle. For each dome was virtually self-contained, taking its heating requirements from the sun. There was no gas; no high-ampage electricity. There were no open fires in the homes. By a policy of living design each house provided safe power, sufficient for its needs.

Perhaps Earth City had become complacent, for now it had no way of fighting fire caused by other means. In fact, except for Hawkwind music, it had no defences of war at all, for it had always been assumed that no enemy other than the Death Generator remained on Earth.

They moved rapidly between the burning domes, surveying the destruction. The ground was littered with debris, the dead and the dying. They came across signs that the effects of displacement were stepping up. Here and there were houses that had apparently escaped the fire but instead, chunks of their structure had gone missing, as though eaten away by invisible mouths.

In places, large pits had been bitten out of the ground. Strange objects from other eras and worlds had been spawned, contrasting oddly with the debris and buildings they were among. Some, like ancient war tanks, were recognizable. Others were totally alien and incomprehensible.

The Hawklords rose into the sky to a avoid a dense column of black smoke which billowed from a cluster of domes. Then they dropped down into the quieter, unburnt southern sector of the City. They landed in the roadway in front of the Dome of Machines, where they hoped to find the Dealer and the Boss.

The dome doors were tightly closed and they had to park their machines in its shadow, away from the glare of fire in the sky. The Sonic Prince ran to the doors. He passed his hand, with the blazing jewel, over their locking mechanisms and they slid smoothly open, revealing a brightly-lit interior.

Two wild and desperate figures stood in the door frame. They were armed with fenders that they had ripped off Starstreakers. One, the larger, held a cassette playing Hawkwind music, which he kept pressed close to his head. The other pointed a small derringer pistol at them.

WILD AUGUR

"Prince!" the larger of the two figures suddenly exclaimed. It was the Boss. The figure with him was a worn and weary version of the Dealer.

Evidently much relieved, the two men lowered their weapons.

"So you made it!" the Dealer said. He looked grateful. "Sorry, but we had to be sure it was you. We're glad you got here, boys." He extended his arm and slapped them on the back as they entered. "We've been expecting you. Come on in."

They entered and he moved past them. His eyes cast themselves anxiously about outside in the flickering street. His manner was such that he urged them to hurry deeper into the central chamber of the dome, away from the doors.

But the Baron restrained him.

"Don't worry," he told him. "They won't be bothering us now."

The Dealer looked puzzled, and the Hawklord explained what they had done.

"So it was you who turned the bloody music off!" the Boss shouted accusingly. He held up the cassette player which he was using to keep himself upright. "I'm not sorry you managed to do it, though," he added. His grimy face looked almost cheerful. His illness appeared to have left him and he seemed oddly at home in the extreme conditions as though all along he had been waiting for them to occur. There was no doubt that he was at his best during emergencies, and once he got going his ability to bring himself and the whole band through them was phenomenal. "But you'll still have to shut the doors…Move in!" he yelled at them. He pushed his way past them to activate the door mechanisms.

Hound Master looked alarmed.

"We can't stay in here long, Boss. We'll get burned!"

"Long enough to work out what we've got to do," the other replied. "I'm not letting any of those little ghouls in from outside."

"Well just remember that we're not magicians!" the Captain declared. "We can't stop the City burning. And I've got no idea at all how we're going to tackle it...unless we let it die down on its own."

"If we do that, we put the small part of the City that's left unburnt in jeopardy!" the Hound Master cried. "We must think of a way."

But he could think of none. He moved unwillingly into the central chamber where, only days ago, they had first set out on their Starstreakers. Things had seemed bad enough at the time; now they seemed a thousand times worse. Recklessly, he found himself thinking of abandoning the City altogether and returning to search for the Life Sword. It seemed pointless to waste time rebuilding their numbers when the Death Generator still existed to knock them down again. With the sword they could cut the cancer out of the planet's heart. He knew, however, that his feelings were unrealistic. They had to find a way of getting the Children back to their feet. They had to find Patti...

First, they had to find a way of stopping the fire...

But it blazed on, spreading from building to building, its hunger never satisfied.

The Hawklords paced agitatedly between the open hatches in the floor. All the machinery normally stored inside seemed to have been pulled out and lay in disarray, as though it had been tested for possible use as weaponry and then discarded.

"What happened?" the Crystal Princess softly asked the Boss and the Dealer. In their anxiety to combat the fire they had forgotten to ask what had caused it.

"The kids went bloody bonkers, that's what!" the Boss told her as he sealed the inner doors. He stood on guard in front of them. "Don't ask me how — we didn't have a chance to find out. They weren't drunk; not that there's any drink around..."

"It started just after you left," the Dealer added. "We think we know what caused it, but we're not sure now. Everything happened so fast. There was a looney who wandered in from the desert..."

"A nutter!" the Boss interjected.

"He seemed to like the music," the Dealer continued. "You boys must be more famous than I thought," he added sardonically. "He came out of the desert and began screaming at us, but at first I didn't take any notice. I thought he was one of the kids who'd done a spell on his own. He lived with us a couple of days and didn't bother us much...just ran around the City waving his sword. He had a bloody great sword from somewhere. Then he tried to break into the Time Vault." The Dealer looked helplessly at their expressions of alarm. "We couldn't stop him! He wasn't affected by our music, so our music guns were useless. The kids were too weak to fight. We had a go at him, but we couldn't get past his sword. I *fired* at him and the bullet just stopped short in front of him...that's when I realized he was no kid! He was protected by some kind of force shield, but it wasn't anything to do with the Death Generator. If it had been he wouldn't have been able to stand our music. Then he broke in the vault. He said that was where he wanted to be...next to the gear and wait for you."

"Wait for us?" Captain Calvert asked.

"Yeah. Don't ask me what for. We couldn't make out what he said most of the time, he was so far gone." He paused and looked thoughtfully at them. "Looking back, maybe he wasn't so much far gone as weighed down. He looked really screwed up by something. He didn't seem to take any offence to my bullet either. He *looked* like he was in despair."

"Maybe he came to us to get help," suggested the Crystal Princess. She looked almost concerned.

"No chance of that! He broke in the Time Vault, then the next day — this morning to be precise — he came running out on stage, raving again. He really flipped this time, and that's when the kids started to get affected. They got excited and began tearing the place apart! We appealed to this guy to stop whatever it was he was doing to them but we couldn't get through to him. Then the kids started attacking us and we had to fight our way in here. It was either that or finish them all off, and we didn't want to do that." He gestured vaguely outside the dome walls and shuddered. They could hear the isolated shouts and explosions muffled by the walls. "I didn't expect this," he continued, looking downcast. "The cards seemed to have given up on me lately. Ever since the Generator stepped up its power I just can't make head or tail of them at all!" He stuck his thumbs under his braces and walked sadly over to his table, shaking his head at the disarrayed cards that lay on its surface.

The Hawklords looked distraught.

"This guy, he must be some manifestation of the Generator's" the Baron spoke.

"Then how come he can stand up to our music?" the Sonic Prince asked him.

The Baron shot him an accusing glance. "Maybe you don't remember those mutants that Mephis once sent us, but I do!"

The unpleasant memory returned to them.

The few remaining Children and the Hawklord had been gathered on Parliament Hill, waiting for their end to come, surrounded by the devastating effects of the Death Concentrator which had been used by Mephis to concentrate the Death Generator's lethal rays. Their music had fought back the front of Darkness and although Mephis had been unable to invade their stronghold, they had been unable to get out to escape. Any agent of Mephis would have died instantly beneath the effects of the Hawkwind music.

Their satanic bodies would have exploded into jelly. However, agents *had* been sent in, under hypnosis by the Dark Lord. Their bodies had fallen to bits even as they fought.

"That's all the more reason to find out who he is...!" the Hound Master exclaimed. "If he put a spell on the Children we might be able to get him to take it off them again. Then we can get the music back on and raise the manpower to tackle these fires."

"Good idea!" the Boss retorted. "It's getting too hot in here for my liking." He fanned himself with the cassette which he still held close to his head, absorbing its healing rays. From it, came a rather tinny, uneven sound due to the buckled spools and bad make of amplifier, but it kept him upright and it was no reflection at all on the powerful, moody Hawkwind track *Steppenwolf* which it now tried to render.

"To the hill!" said the Dealer, reaching for the cigar in his mouth. But it wasn't there.

BLADE OF ANARCHY

Nothing was there.

Gradually they were being stripped of the things they had carved out of the desert...and the desert and the nothingness was returning to claim them. The mutinous crowds had been subdued.

The fire had died down somewhat, unable to spread across the once pleasant gardens and squares that divided the City. But the larger part of Earth City was still wildly ablaze, the flames undying and the smoke forming a thick, choking haze that partly obscured the flames. Bodies of the Children lay in the roadways, motionless and dead, but many had evidently arisen to escape the flames and were withstanding the extreme effects.

The Hawklords flew past the horrendous scenes, filled with grief and bitterness.

Parliament Hill looked dismal and grey in the smoke-filled night. Its lights were all but extinguished, and its huge stage tarnished. The shapes of the Children had moved away from the stage area altogether and looked passively on; frighteningly silent in their suffering. The Hawklords ignored their listless gazes and glided towards the box-like Time Vault where their equipment lay stored and where, according to the Dealer, the lone pilgrim had taken himself.

The shining black wall of the cube building loomed up in the swirling smoke. Soon they were standing outside its closed doors, angry that its mechanism had been tampered with and the sacrosanct musical armoury inside invaded. At a knock the doors swung apart, their time locks broken, and they were able to see inside the blackened interior.

"Wherever you are, show yourself" the Sonic Prince called out.

The dim outlines of the cabinets that contained the Hawkwind instruments and the rectangular and triangular shapes of the electronic hardware that had been hastily drawn in by the roadies, gradually became visible. It proved impossible to detect anything else.

The Prince stood in the mouth of the door, armed with the Dealer's derringer. At his side stood the Boss, holding on to a metal bar for luck. The five other Hawklords peered over their shoulders, their bodies glowing menacingly.

"We know you're in there!" the Boss shouted. "Come out or we'll come in and get you!"

A black area somewhere at the back of the room moved.

Instinctively, they drew back. Something glinted in the dark and a demonic howling sound swept through the air. A tall, lean shape sprang towards them and burst abruptly into the open doorway. In its hand it held an immense sword that seemed to live of its own accord, cutting and slashing at the air, the like of which none had seen before.

Now the figure could be clearly seen in the hellish fire glow that suffused through the smoke clouds, and they fell farther back in terror. It was taller than them by a head and shoulders, and clad lightly in armour. It had a sickly-white face and long, strangely virile hair that gleamed silvery-white. Its eyes were most alarming of all. They were narrow and seemed to be buried inside the skull. They were set so deeply back, they burned sullenly like tiny vermilion stones.

"Who are you?" gasped the Sonic Prince in horror. An invisible force, neither good nor evil, radiated on the Hawklords and they knew that the apparition was not of Earth.

At the Prince's words the black sword in its hand began humming and it writhed more strongly yet to escape its wielder's grasp, its point aimed dead at the Hawklord's heart.

A battle seemed to be going on between master and blade, and the figures's skull-like face twisted with conflict.

"Back, hell-blade!" he hissed, and with a final howl the great sword was forced to withdraw. The Hawklords watched gladly as it was returned to its jewel-encrusted scabbard.

The figure looked up at them with its burning, tormented eyes and held them in its gaze.

Its cruel thin lips curled back and its chin tilted.

"I am Elric of Meniboné!" it declared proudly, making the Hawklords gasp in outright amazement.

They stared in awe at the hero whose adventures they knew so well.

BORN TO GO

On the cold and almost lifeless deserts of Earth, glowing shapes moved like spectres, busying themselves on their nocturnal mission. The shape that was the Light Lord bent down and effortlessly hefted his Starstreaker into an upright position. The machine glinted in the starlight. It was built out of the lightest alloys, though it was still heavy to a mortal's grasp.

Looking around him to check that the others were ready, he swung himself across its frame and into his seat. Then he snapped the hand bar shut in front of him. It lay across his middle, holding him in and providing a grip for his hands. Most importantly of all it acted as a power conductor, transferring the full power of his mind to the psycotronic engine.

He gripped the bar tightly, and concentrated. Gradually, Hawklord and machine became a new creature.

It rose slowly, gracefully, into the night.

The other three craft behind him had also risen and he guided himself into their loose formation.

"If everyone's ready we'll get going," Thunder Rider's irritated voice called out to them. They could make out his goggled face peering round at them through the dark.

The Light Lord grinned perversely. After the extraordinary event that had taken place in the desert they had ragged the Hawklord unmercifully. Obviously there was nothing funny about what had happened as far as Thunder Rider was concerned. They had been resting, waiting for the first light so that they could continue their search. Without warning, the red-haired saxophonist had started screaming and rolling about, fighting and scratching at the sand. Then he had sprung to his feet and ran off into the night, yelling out obscenities.

His behaviour had taken them totally by surprise and at first they had sat speechlessly, wondering what had prompted it. Then they had followed the Hawklord to bring him back. They had found him miles away to the east, half-naked, peeling off his clothes and casting them to the winds.

"Ready as we'll ever be!" smiling Lord Rudolph told Thunder Rider.

"Sure you can find your way this time?" Astral Al asked him. There was a tone of amusement in his voice also.

In reality, there was little that was comical in their predicament. After the visitation by the mysterious Red Queen, the uncomfortable thought that their actions were no longer produced of their own free will, that perhaps, as the Dealer had tried to warn, Patti and Lord Jefferson's disappearance had been engineered, was confirmed.

The Light Lord stabbed a button in front of him and Hawkwind music began flooding out into the blackness. It was *City of Lagoons*, another of their numbers from the *Astounding Sounds, Amazing Music* album, composed just before the final collapse of the old civilization. The album had marked a departure from their earlier music. They had introduced many new themes while retaining the best ingredients of the old, already semi-aware of the world changes to come and the musical strength they would need. Since that time they had composed very little; partly because there were more pressing needs to fulfil, and partly because the Children preferred to listen to the older numbers.

Now, new music was needed again, and providing they got through their ordeals alive they planned, on their return, to re-open the Time Vault and begin composing.

They journeyed on across the desert, following Thunder Rider's meandering spore across the sand with the aid of lamps attached to their craft.

Then, in the darkness ahead, they noticed the vast bulk of the Time Fault.

It stretched away in the starlight to the east. This part of the fault lay a good distance from where they had searched earlier in the day and the tracks in the sand were more easy to follow. About a quarter of a mile in front of them lay the Time Zone itself.

It bulged out ominously into the desert, larger than its neighbouring Zones, growing like a fat, cancerous tumour along the parent stem.

Malice emanated from it and they approached cautiously into its field of influence. They felt their minds dissolving in the invisible rays that came off it — rays that were far stronger than those of the other Time Zones.

"It wasn't this size before," Thunder Rider remarked.

They flew as close to it as they dared, and brought their machines down to the ground. The saxophonist dismounted and walked across the sand towards it.

Close up, it looked like jelly, like a grotesquely enlarged frogspawn, though it did not quiver.

Dark and foreboding, it looked cold and lifeless. He knew that the energies locking inside it were sufficient, if released at once, to shatter the Earth.

He bent down to retrieve the belt he had dropped as a marker. A glimmer of light appeared in the Time Zone wall.

The light grew stronger and began to gleam threateningly. Simultaneously, a freezing vapour poured from its surface, and the warm air of the desert began to rush in towards it.

"It's absorbing our heat energy!" the Light Lord cried, grasping what was starting to happen.

Thunder Rider leapt back on to his Starstreaker and together the party backed off in alarm.

The hot wind became a howling, shrieking gale. But as they flew away, it abated. Eventually it had become no more than a mild head breeze, sucked across the sands.

They brought their machines around and waited.

The node-like bulge still glowed. Now it shone fiercely cold, and the landscape round about was lit up with an intense glare.

It was visible as a thick, white column inside a jagged, pulsating corolla of light that stretched up into the sky.

As they watched, the light exploded outward.

Then the incandescent mass began to die, but instead of collapsing back in on itself as they expected, its new boundary remained. The bright outline of light dimmed. Soon the Zone looked dark and lifeless once more.

It had grown enormously, claiming even more of the desert and the space it occupied in the Fault, carelessly compressing its neighbours on either side.

Astounded, the Hawklords continued to gaze at the sight long after the explosion of light and cold had subsided. Resolutely, they began to move forward again. Except for chill air rising off the freezing sand, the wind died away altogether. Once more they hovered in front of the Time Zone's motionless surface and felt its mind-scrambling waves, more potent than ever.

"It's OK now…" Astral Al reached out his arms to touch it. Tentatively he poked his gloved finger into it. It felt cold and he withdrew it quickly. They felt their senses dimming.

"I can't hold my mind together much longer!" he complained, clasping his head with his hands.

"Nor I!" Lord Rudolph exclaimed. "We've spent too long delaying…"

"If we're going in, let's go in!" Astral Al cried out.

"Keep together!" Thunder Rider warned them. "In case we don't all get through in the same place."

As one they slid in, unable to hold themselves back any longer.

They felt relief.

Their senses fragmented and they lost awareness except for that of the chaotic images of their past lives. They saw their ghost forms riding together, but though they retained the image for recall, once they had travelled through the Zone wall, they were unable to comprehend them.

The four ghost riders split into a hundred thousand as they marched through Time — a silent army of warriors pushing forward towards the unknown.

HALL OF THE SUPERSTARS

The world was drab and dark.

The air was heavy with the fingers of the Death Radiation. They breathed as though short of breath, but gradually their bodies adapted. They began to collect their senses together.

They had arrived in a large, open hall.

It was bathed in a dim, yet sharply metallic light that seemed to come from nowhere and everywhere. The air shimmered and their bodies glowed fiercely, sending off counter-radiation.

It was a dirty hall, and looked as though it hadn't been used for centuries. Its ceiling was low and supported by metal beams, adding to the claustrophobic effect.

Large, grey cobwebs hung from the struts. On the walls were posters or notices, most of them falling or torn. The floor was littered with smashed glass, paper cups and rubbish from a concert that had been held their long ago.

At one end lay the stage mouth, choked full of stacked chairs and crates. At the other stood a decrepit-looking bar. The air smelt musty and faintly acrid.

"What happened to this place?" Thunder Rider shuddered.

"What happened to the whole age, you mean!" Lord Rudolph muttered in dismay. He ran his fingers along one of the walls by the side. "It's dust! We've landed in another uninhabitable time!"

"Uninhabited," corrected the Light Lord, gazing about him. "If it were uninhabitable we wouldn't be standing here now — not for long anyway." He dismounted from his Starstreaker and walked slowly forward across the floor, his boots kicking aside the debris.

Lord Rudolph felt depressed. He stared at the stomping figure with the look of a man deranged. They had expected to find a world in which their offspring might plausibly have lived.

"Where's 'here'?" Thunder Rider asked, equally morose. "The Red Queen…we didn't find this place by chance, you know."

"Could be a trap," Astral Al agreed. He looked uncertainly at the decayed interior. It looked similar to the ruins that had once stood at the end of the Pre-Dawn era when they had first staged their war against the Dark Forces and Memphis Mephis had stalked the Earth. Perhaps they had been returned to fight him again.

Cautiously they slid their music guns from their holsters. They began to edge away from the invisible Zone wall behind them and follow the Light

Lord. He moved ahead of their machines, on foot. Occasionally he stooped to collect some artifact or other from the floor to examine it, only to toss it back into the dust again.

"Dead," he commented. "It's not been occupied or played in for years."

He reached the far side of the hall and brought his hand up to one of the poster-like papers affixed to the wall, but it crumbled away. He flicked on his lamp and a mercury light spilled through the gloom, lighting up the faces of long dead rock stars and their bands. They were the legendary rock bands of the late Nineteen Sixties and Seventies: Jefferson Airplane, The Grateful Dead, Santana, Jimi Hendrix, The Rolling Stones, Janis Joplin, Pink Floyd, Captain Beefheart...The Hawklord whistled in amazement. "Unbelievable!" he exclaimed, reeling off their names. The other Hawklord crowded round. "They don't seem to be from any particular date either, just mementoes from visiting bands..."

"Here's one of us!" Thunder Rider pointed, momentarily aroused from his despondency. "HAWKWIND," he read out. "LIVE AT ALPHA CENTAURA...That's a new one on me!"

"Me too," Lord Rudolph remarked. 'Pity it doesn't say what the venue was."

"It's got a date — 1971, so that's when we must have played it...if we ever did."

"Most of them seem to be from around that time," the Light Lord observed, peering at the posters. "1972 seems to be about the latest. Maybe the hall shut down then. They all seem to advertise different venues..." He sounded puzzled. "Avalon Ballroom, Longshoreman's Hall, Fillmore West..."

"Decoration perhaps?" Astral Al suggested casually. But he didn't feel as calm as he looked. The dead hall had a haunting effect on him. It seemed like an old photograph in the strange lighting. It looked familiar, as though somewhere in his immortal mind lay the corresponding picture, waiting to be dredged out. His mental feelers couldn't probe the right places. There were too many memories in between now and then.

On impulse, he leaned down from his Starstreaker and picked up one of the many paper cups that had been discarded on the floor. Its thick waxed sides had a greater resistance to the erosions of time, and he blew away the dust. Beneath the grime was a picture of snow-capped mountains. A clown's happy face hung in the sky, representing the sun. Beneath the mountains were people walking around in sunglasses, families with children, cars and amusements. Lettering ran around the base of the cup, designed to look as though it had been carved out of ice: PLAYLAND WELCOME TO PLAYLAND WELCOME TO...

He stared intently at the words.

A flood of memories came. Their power shook him.

He tossed the cup to Thunder Rider. "Take a decco," he said.

Anxiously the Hawklords drifted towards the object captured in Thunder Rider's hands. They clustered around as close to each other as they could get on their machines, and shone their lamps on it.

"Playland," the Light Lord spelt out. "Means nothing to me."

The other two Hawklords looked equally puzzled.

"What's it mean?" Thunder Rider asked Astral Al.

"You've heard of it. It's just that you don't remember," the other replied. "Maybe if I said 'Family Dog' you'd cotton on…"

"*Playland!*" Thunder Rider exclaimed. "That's in San Francisco…!"

"*Was* in San Francisco," Astral Al corrected him. "That is unless *this* is San Francisco…Playland was near the last Family Dog rock auditorium. It was just like this one…"

Now they could remember the famous site that had lain on the West Coast of California. In its time it had been one of Frisco's great venues for Rock Bands. However, they hadn't gigged there themselves.

"Playland was pulled down…" began Lord Rudolph. "I distinctly remember. It was pulled down in…" He broke off, an alarmed expression appearing on his face. "We must have arrived *before* it was pulled down. We're too early for Mephis…and too early for Death Rays." He shivered. "You know what that means, don't you?"

They needed no prompting.

"We've not arrived in our own Time Stream at all," Thunder Rider voiced their thoughts. "That must mean we're in one of the alternative Earths…an Earth taken over by the Dark Forces!"

"It would make sense," the Light Lord commented. "If the Red Queen is in league with them."

"If she would only show herself again, I'd feel a lot better," Thunder Rider said. 'We would have something tangible to fight."

"Our object is not to fight, but to save our Children," Lord Rudolph said. "Let's get them and get out!"

Before anyone could comment further, a note of music sounded from somewhere within the derelict hall. It was a melodic, unearthly sound and they peered around, trying vainly to detect where it came from or what it was.

"The Vulvaphone!" Thunder Rider shouted, first to recognize the blissful strains of the instrument that he and Patti had fashioned.

Excitedly, he dismounted from his Starstreaker. He gently lifted the magical instrument from where he had strapped it at the back of his machine. Under the wistful gaze of Lord Rudolph who had drifted round, he opened its protective crystal casement. Both Hawklords could see perfectly well through the casement that the instrument inside was functioning. They needed to watch the delicate strings vibrating against the bone discs at close quarters.

They watched, entranced by the thought of Patti's unseen mouth blowing down the mouthpiece; her psychic empathy activating its delicate mechanisms.

"While she's alive, we'll keep this instrument plugged in," Lord Rudolph vowed.

Thunder Rider nodded. Tremulously, lest he damage it, he placed the Vulvaphone back in its case and re-strapped it on its rest. He separated the wires that led from it to the amplification equipment mounted on his Starstreaker and clipped them down so they couldn't accidentally be jerked out.

He felt the Hawk-power course through his being.

"Let's go and find them!" he cried exaltedly. "Trap or not!"

He remounted his Starstreaker and played his music gun into the air. A jagged bolt of light sprang from it as the music reacted with the increased level of the Death Rays. A loud report filled the dismal hall and the smell of ozone rose on the air.

The Light Lord returned to his machine, and together the silent craft drifted like glowing ghosts across the ancient dance-floor. The hall had once rang with the optimistic music of the rock bands, and the wild applause of their fans. At one time, perhaps, the hall had belonged to their own era, then mysteriously split off and followed an alternate Time Stream of its own. The hall had then been abandoned by the happy throngs and left to decay in the eternal twilight.

THE MACHINERIES OF JOY

The memories seemed a long time ago. Now they rose freely, unbidden inside Astral Al's head as he crashed his Starstreaker against the door marked "EXIT." The door cracked open with ease, leaving a cloud of dust where it had stood and he led their machines out into the dark, uninviting passageway behind.

They came to a maze of confusing alleys, each as dreary and empty of life as the hall had been.

"We must remember our way back, otherwise we're gonners!" Lord Rudolph reminded them as they went. Despite the oppression, he was back to his usual cheery self. If Patti were alive, that meant there was a good chance of him finding his son alive also.

They drifted up short flights of stairs and down again into different parts of the building. Eventually they arrived at a foyer, still lit by the stark, bluish light.

More debris met their gaze, only here, the destruction was worse. It seemed as though the entire front of the building had been semi-demolished by a combination of Time and the efforts of vandals or workmen who had long since fled their jobs. Garbage bags had been tipped amongst the rubble, the contents now dried and musty, and heaps of what looked like air rifles and decayed boxes had been dumped carelessly in one corner. Then, after choking up its mouth, it seemed that the last inhabitants had left the hall to its fate.

Through the glass doors they caught sight of the outside. The glass had been broken, and they could see through clearly, but because of the uniformity of the light and the lack of shadow, it seemed that the outside was merely a larger extension of the interior. It was a scene they half expected.

But as they burst through the flimsy doors they gazed on a vista of wreckage and destruction that seemed beyond comprehension.

"That's Playland," Thunder Rider commented softly.

The once famous pleasure complex, of which the hall was only a part, lay all around them.

Whirlitzers, the Octopus, the Fun House, a Roller Coaster, Dodgem cars and penny arcades — all the machineries of joy that had once been a favourite escape of the human race — lay in glorious dissolution. The massive steel supports that supported the Roller Coaster cars were only just fulfilling their functions, eaten away by rust and in places already falling into parts of the decaying fairground. The Ferris Wheel had toppled from its position and now lay on its side, barely recognizable beneath the twisted girders, brown rust and masonry. The Octopus was leaning perilously against the Giant Barrel and the Dodgem cars had been taken from their enclosure and scattered at random. Where natural elements hadn't yet done their work, human ones had, for the ruins themselves had been physically stirred about.

The Hawklords felt a sense of loneliness and desolation fall on them — far greater than anything they had experienced in the deserts. Seeing the disarray of familiar objects they had once taken for granted in a time similar to the one they had once called their own, filled them with despair. But the damning light that effused sluggishly out of everywhere was a more horrific evoker of memory.

"It reminds me of the world as it was under Mephis!" Thunder Rider said. "The poor sods who lived here — I pity them."

"If Patti's here…" began the Light Lord.

'Don't say that!" Lord Rudolph smiled. "Don't say 'if'! She *is* in here, and we'll find her…and my son!"

"Sorry," the Light Lord apologized. "I merely meant to ask how we were going to set about finding her. We aren't getting much help from the Red Queen, whoever she is. Not that we want that from her."

"There must be something else here other than ruins," Thunder Rider said. He squinted into the distance. "Patti must be held somewhere in it. I don't know much about San Francisco, but if this is Playland we should be able to see the Pacific Ocean."

Astral Al shifted uncomfortably. More of the memories inside him coincided with details outside. He pointed to a thin line of slightly lighter substance on the dismal horizon. "Is that it?" he asked.

The others looked intently at the line.

"Could be," Thunder Rider said.

"Then the residential area's over there, I think," Astral Al gestured to one side. "That's where we're going to find life, if there is any."

"We can give it a try." Lord Rudolph looked faintly puzzled by Astral Al's unusual powers, but he did not pursue the matter. "We'd only go around in circles here."

In silent agreement they guided their machines away from the doomed building, into the demolished landscape.

Perpetual twilight reigned. They meandered through the deserted amusement arcades, past a grisly set of giant-sized doll-like dummies of clowns and other specimens of humanity, at one time used to arouse laughter but now far from funny.

They came to the leaning Octopus, its still extended arms clutching the silent passenger seats. In the dimness it looked like a giant, paralyzed insect of metal. It could never again move; only the thoughts of unease it brought to their minds had any power now.

They moved past it, scanning the shadowless landscape, followed by the ethereal notes of the Vulvaphone.

They saw a light. It flickered briefly on and off, as more wreckage came between it and the moving Hawklords. They retraced their steps and located it again. It lay off their course, a single beam of white light, a lone sign of life amongst the desolate ruins.

BLACK CARAPICE

The phosphorescent bodies of the Hawklords began to rise silently astride the Starstreakers.

They climbed until they were able to clear the tallest of the projections from below, and then began to coast along in the direction of the light.

It still lay a good distance from them, towards where they thought the coast lay. As they neared it they heard music. It was not the music of the

Vulvaphone, but that of an accordion.

It was old-fashioned country music, totally out of place in the abandoned, death landscape.

The Hawklords glanced at one another in puzzlement and suspicion.

The point of light grew larger. It seemed to emanate from one of the fairground machines. Cautiously, they increased their speed. Then, another noise sounded in the background. It was like the roar of motorbike engines.

The engine noises stopped, and the accordion continued playing on its own. It played a square dance, and now they could hear the caller's name shouting out instructions.

"Dozee do, and round again!" the voice shouted merrily. "Backs to the wall, swing your partners round and round..."

They were able to see the illuminated machinery clearly now — a Waltzer, in full swing, empty seats, swivelling around with the lights and music blazing out from it. Though evidently intact and moving, it seemed as abandoned and empty as the wreckage.

They reduced their height further, moving slowly forward between the outcrops of rubble to avoid being seen.

Abruptly, the music ceased.

The Hawklords stopped, and peered through the rubbish.

They could see the pained Waltzer clearly now, and hear the squeaking of its seats and the rumble of its undulating floor as it swept around.

As they watched, it gradually slowed down to a halt. There was a moment of complete silence, then from the far side of the Waltzer they heard gruff American voices arguing. The voices rose. There came a soft thudding sound, followed by a groan.

"You disobeyed!" one voice said. There came another thud, and another agonized groan. "Now we'll make sure you keep off the juice line!" the same voice said.

"Uh!" a voice screamed. "Uhhhh! Uhhhh!" There were more blows.

The Hawklords veered upward on their machines.

"Whoever is getting the punches is getting murdered!" Thunder Rider exclaimed. "We've got to stop them."

They streaked down toward the Waltzer and flew rapidly around its perimeter. They were brought up suddenly by the scene that met them.

Three mutant humans were fighting. Their skins were deformed, their faces bubbled into blisters and marked with deep, weeping sores. In swollen sockets and extrusions of flesh, their eyes and mouths were scarcely visible.

Two of the figures evidently were motorcycle policemen, and they were beating up the other.

They were dressed in dark blue riding breeches and black leather jackets, black gloves and boots, and big black holsters with revolvers with ivory butts.

One held the fallen mutant whist the other hit him with the barrel of his gun. The gun rose repeatedly in the air and descended on the bloated face. From the scene led a beaten roadway, passing between banks of the rubbish which had been strewn to each side. At the neck of the road where it entered the clearing were two massive fully-dressed Harley Davidsons with tall, wide windshields, radios, bulky saddles and knee shields.

At sight of the four Hawklords, the Bulls let the fairgroundsman drop to the ground and brought up their revolvers.

"Stay where you are!" one of them ordered.

The Hawklords brought their machines to rest on the ground, and the guns erupted in front of them.

Bullets smashed their way into the Starstreakers.

"I said stay still!" the Bull shouted, enraged. It was difficult to see what expression they wore under the gross distortions.

Astral Al, in common with the other three Hawklords felt an instant repulsion. They had encountered such creatures in their last battle with the Dark Forces. He drew himself up to his full height.

"Guns don't frighten the Hawklords!" he cried. His helmeted figure in its sleek battle costume looked a forbidding sight but the two creatures in front of him seemed not to notice his power.

As the Starstreakers began bearing down on them, the Bulls began firing their guns again, ineffectively against the strong visors. The Hawklord stabbed their buttons on the hand-bars in front of them, activating the powerful music cannons mounted on their hoods. A screech of Hawkwind tracks began blaring out of the small, uni-directional nozzles.

Brainstorm, Orgone Accumulator, Sonic Attack...

As their notes hit the bluish plasma that passed for air, white sparks were produced that leapt towards the Bulls. The burly policemen staggered under the onslaught and fell bodily to the ground, twitching convulsively.

Soon they lay perfectly still.

The Hawklords switched their weaponry off, and dismounted. Pungent ozone, produced by the sparking, drifted in the air and rose up their nostrils. They strode over to the prone bodies and kicked them to make sure they were dead.

"I've met some good coppers in my time, I must admit," Lord Rudolph remarked.

"They're probably only a sampling of what to expect in this world," Thunder Rider added.

The figure of the fairgroundsman stirred on the floor. It sat up groggily and stared at them with its bloodied face and great folds of skin. It looked like a gruesome sight, and their first instinct was to leave it to its fate. But they were stirred by feelings of pity.

Distastefully, Thunder Rider and the Light Lord took hold of its arms and helped raise it to its feet.

"You OK?" Thunder Rider asked it. The creature looked at them blankly. It began heaving. Weakly it raised its arm and pointed to the Waltzer. With soundless gestures it guided them to the control box at the centre of the fairground machine. Inside, they found a mess of amplifiers, wires, food cartons, magazine cuttings and a mattress covered with old blankets. They laid the mutant down where it wanted to go. Almost immediately it fell unconscious and the two Hawklords stood around helplessly wondering what they could do to treat its wounds. The mass of blister-like pads its skin had degenerated into seemed to have protected it from the worst blows, but it still looked in a bad way.

"Best leave him and hope he wakes up," the Light Lord said.

Reluctantly, Thunder Rider agreed, and they rejoined the other two Hawklords outside.

"If they're still here when we get back, we're taking them with us!" Lord Rudolph was saying. He and Astral Al were gazing enviously at the two motorbikes mounted on their side stands. "Patti and Lord Jefferson can ride them back!"

'We've no fuel for engines like that," the Light Lord commented as he overheard them.

"That's no worry, Light Lord!" Astral Al replied, running his gloved hand over a petrol tank. "It'd be worth taking them back just for what you'd get out of one tankful…!"

Static from one of the bikes interrupted him, and a voice burst out: "You there, Mac?" it said. "We got a…" Thunder Rider leaned forward towards the bike. He located the radio control amongst the accessories and tore out the main wire. The set went dead. He walked over to the other bike and performed the same operation.

"Just make sure they don't get traced."

OVENS OF DEATH

Now they were able to follow a road the Hawklords made faster progress. They streaked without having to watch for the jagged girders and fingers of masonry that projected from the machine cemetery that lay beneath them.

The road leading from the derelict Playland and its solitary eccentric who still lived there took them southeast, in the direction of central San Francisco.

"We should come to a zoo first," Astral Al informed them, "in Golden Gate

Park."

They reached the edge of the ruins. They had been fenced off with a high wall of corrugated iron. A doorway in the wall left open by the Bulls enabled them to survey the scene outside before leaving. The same bluish light bathed everywhere, making it difficult to pick out features. Although unnaturally clear, it made the land look as though it were bathed in a kind of moonlight, destroying its natural colouring.

Beyond them they could see the silent cages and walkways of the zoo, apparently empty of life, though for some strange reason not derelict.

"We better close the gates behind us," Lord Rudolph said. "Just in case anyone happens along."

The gates squeaked on their hinges as they pulled them to. Then the Hawklords set off across the cracked concrete surface in front of them.

They followed Astral Al between the cages and the walled-off pits and enclosures. As they passed them they heard shuffling and clanking sounds and noticed that animals of some kind were tethered inside. The animals were packed ten or twenty to a cage and apart from the noises of their movement they made no other sounds.

"They don't seem to be asleep," Thunder Rider observed, peering in at some of them. He looked more closely, then he stepped back in shock, "They're not animals! They're mutant slaves of some kind!"

"Or prisoners. I doubt if slaves could work in their condition," the Light Lord noted, peering in. Above the metallic tang of the air they could now detect the stench of putrescence and biological decay, recognizable in any world. The chained mutants were unclothed, their festering skin exposed, causing them to appear at first glance like animals.

The Hawklords wrinkled their noses and felt sick.

"Can't we let them out?" Lord Rudolph asked. "They could at least wash themselves..."

Before they could decide, a drone of engines sounded in the distance.

They flew gratefully away from the cages and found a place to hide in a narrow passageway between two animal houses. From here they had a clear view of the cages and the roadway.

The roar of the bike engines increased, and soon three more 1200CC Harley Davidsons appeared, speeding towards them. The heavy machines skidded to a halt in front of them. The Hawklords remained perfectly motionless, hoping that they wouldn't be seen. Much as they were beginning to hate certain occupants in this world, they wanted to save their energy and luck for rescuing Patti.

The Bulls dismounted and pulled keys from their pockets. In their black gloves they carried gadgets of some kind. They slouched purposefully, like uniformed gorillas, towards the cages and began opening the barred doors. The once-human creatures inside shuffled and began moaning. Instead of trying to escape, they shrank further to the back of their cages. One of the police mutants made a taunting sound.

"The kiddies are shy today," he said. "Let's see what a bit of music does for them!" He chuckled and looked down at the gadget he held in his hand. Then he depressed a button.

The watching Hawklords shot startled looks at each other. Before they could react, the alien music was upon them. Its throbbing waves beat at their bodies, as though with physical blows. They began falling from their Starstreakers, unable to retain their co-ordination.

All three tape-recorders were now being played, and at the edges of their departing senses the Hawklords recognized the strains of the rival pop songs: *Nights In White Satin*, by the Moody Blues; *Sounds of Silence*, by Simon and Garfunkel; *Bohemian Rhapsody*, by Queen…all mixed in a clashing, roaring, dissolving mass.

"We've…got…to…stop…them…!" Thunder Rider gasped. He reached forward slowly as though in a nightmare and pressed weakly against the button that activated the Starstreaker's music cannon. But his vital Hawk power had drained away, and he could not press it. "P-R-E-S-S, FUCK YOU!!!" he whispered hoarsely. He punched out savagely with his remaining power.

From somewhere by his side a jagged spark leapt out. Hawkwind music flooded over his being. His strength returned, and he smiled weakly at the Light Lord.

"Good on you. We'd have been gonners…" he gasped. He switched on his own music system and the powerful speakers above him began to add to the growing power. Soon, the narrow passageway in which they sat was ablaze with crackling light. The light forced its way out of both ends of the vent and the Bulls turned and watched the scene with blank, ugly faces. Their own power was now ebbing and pointed their tape-recorders at the Hawklords too late.

The Hawklords filed out into the open, deflecting the Death music as they rode, and began to train their apparatus directly on the Bulls.

The two kinds of music energy clashed in a ball of light. They drew on both the conflicting energies of the Death Generator and the delatronized Hawkwind music. The mutants in the cages shied away from the spectacle, gurgling in fear. The superior power of the four mounted music cannons of the Hawklords, playing *Kerb Crawler*, *City of Lagoons*, *Reefer Madness* and *Chronoglide Skyway* gradually forced the white-hot ball of light towards the three policeman in a triumphant combination of sound. The Bulls sank to their knees, aiming their tape recorders in front of them and trying vainly to turn their volume controls higher. Still aiming their guns they began walking towards their bikes on knee-caps. But their efforts were fruitless.

Screaming, they collapsed forward, engulfed by the light.

"That was close!" Lord Rudolph gasped.

The Hawklords turned off their equipment and surveyed the charred bodies at their feet.

"I'll kill the radio," the Light Lord told them, turning away. He began kicking at the bikes with his boots. The others drifted across on their Starstreakers towards the open cages.

"They might be able to tell us something," the Light Lord said hopefully. The mutants were still at the back of their cages, and he called to them to come forward. His words had little effect on them. At sight of him they tried to press themselves even harder against the wall. They seemed totally subordinated, little more than the animals the Hawklords had first supposed them to be.

Annoyed by their stupidity, the Light Lord ventured inside the cage and the grunts and shrieks started up again.

"We've not come to hurt you!" he cried in exasperation. Then he stopped short. Once more there was another painful fact to learn.

The mouths of the creatures were fully open and he could see that they had no tongues. In fact, he noticed, their tongues had been ripped out, for only swollen bumps bobbed about near the backs of their throats.

"Christ!" he shouted in disgust "This is an abysmal world!" He emerged, shaking his head. "I had hoped to find at least one example of resistance. But there's nothing, except perhaps for that fairgroundsman."

"There must be others, Light Lord," Thunder Rider told him. "But we can't afford to look for them. We must get to Patti, and hope we meet some on the way…"

"Then how are we going to know where to look without talking to someone?" the Light Lord asked agitatedly. "We could spend days here, presuming this Zone is as large inside as it looked from outside. Don't forget it's probably still growing!"

"We must keep going," Lord Rudolph told him.

Astral Al raised his arm suddenly and stopped them from mounting their machines. "The Light Lord's right."

They looked at him attentively.

"What do you mean?" Thunder Rider asked, frowning. "You've been holding something back."

"I didn't tell you before because I wasn't sure of something, but now I am." Al glanced about him. "I used to know a guy who lived in 'Frisco. He was a Marine in the Vietnam War. He got killed…"

"You mean he might…be alive?" Thunder Rider asked.

"Why not?" Astral Al shrugged. "He died in 1974. Playland was in ruins then. They pulled it down and a bit later it got redeveloped…If this Time

Stream split from ours before Playland got developed, it's possible it might have separated before Spike's death. In which case he may be alive...in this Time Stream at any rate."

"Spike?"

"That's the Marine. He tried to get out but they wouldn't let him. Then, right at the end of the war...bang!"

"You might be right," the Light Lord spoke thoughtfully. "But supposing this Time Stream is completely different to our own? Suppose that other versions of Jimi Hendrix and all the rest, including us, flourished parallel with us, and never split at all...?"

"That's a risk we have to take," the drummer commented gravely. "The more I think of it, the more I feel sure he's here, somewhere..."

"Then let's be gone before any more of these jokers pay us a visit," Thunder Rider said derisively.

He kicked at one of the corpses and the charred shape shivered into a heap of bluish-grey dust.

CITY OF PERIL

They journeyed deeper into the Time Zone. Still they encountered no planned resistance to their intrusion and they felt a growing unease. They had no alternative but to press on, encouraged by the singing Vulvaphone and the beck of the mysterious Red Queen.

They moved along grave-like thoroughfares: Stanyon Street, Haight Street...eventually arriving at a house made entirely of painted planks of wood, its colour registering as a deeper shade of the uniform bluish-grey to their eyes.

"Spike's," Astral Al told them. "Looks the same as it's always done, except it used to be red. This whole area was built after the 1906 earthquake and some joker thought he could avoid the same thing happening to his house if he built it with nuts and bolts instead of nails."

He moved ahead of them through the gate, and they followed into a weed-choked garden. Two tall houses with stuccoed fronts stood on either side of the house. They rose higher, sterner-looking than Spike's, contributing to the feeling of disquiet the Hawklords felt. They stopped before a ramshackle, covered porchway.

"Doesn't look like anyone's in," the Light Lord said, peering through one of the windows.

"Ring the bell," Lord Rudolph suggested, balancing his Starstreaker on the porch with his feet.

Astral Al reached out and pressed the bell. At the same instant a loud wailing sound started up behind them.

Hurriedly they turned around.

The sound came from behind, and they realized it was a siren of some kind. A roar of bikes started in the distance.

As the Hawklords waited expectantly, the streets began to fill with the denizens of the drab world. They walked along the pavements like automatons, clothed in dismal garments, with deformed skins, gazing sightlessly ahead of them, ignoring anything of interest. They walked in thousands along the streets until they reached their homes and disappeared from sight.

'Commuters!" the Light Lord whispered. "That siren must have been a work signal!"

The creatures kept rigidly to the pavements. Then, along the roadways came the bikes, driven by more Bulls, seeing that the citizens behaved themselves and kept to their daily schedules. Occasionally, cars — long, shiny Lincolns — swished sleekly by, carrying dignitaries on their unknown missions.

"Reminds me of Work!" Lord Rudolph shivered with distaste. "Remember; we used to do that?"

"They don't even notice us," Astral Al remarked as the mutants passed by.

"They've been conditioned," the Light Lord said, "by the Death Music."

The gate in front of them swung open and a large figure began ambling towards them.

It noticed them and hesitated. Then it continued, evidently deciding to ignore them, the flabby rolls of skin on its face flapping and slapping together. Two tiny eyes embedded in the blisters gazed out. Instinctively, the Hawklords drifted aside on the Starstreakers to let it pass.

"Spike?" Astral Al asked it uncertainly. "Is it you?"

Again the creature hesitated, but again continued, until it reached the door. It lifted up a ham-sized arm grasping a bunch of keys, and inserted one of them into the lock.

"Spike…It's Al…" the drummer dismounted. He pulled off his helmet and walked up behind the mutant. The creature froze, its arm still raised to the lock. Then it spun round.

"Spooks!" it cried. "Get back! Leave me alone." Its arms flayed wildly about, trying to wipe them away. With unexpected strength it knocked Astral Al to the ground.

It turned back to the door once more and with frantic motions began to stab at the lock with the key.

Astral Al picked himself up angrily. "Keep your maulers off me!" he yelled out.

"Come on Al, let's go," Lord Rudolph told him. "It's obviously not your friend…times have changed…"

"No, it's Spike all right," Astral Al said, wiping his lips. He grinned suddenly. "That's just the way he'd behave. Spike!" he yelled out again. "We're not spooks."

He looked down at himself. Their figures rippled and glowed with the Hawklord energy.

The mutant dropped the keys and they clattered to the doorstep. Now it trembled with fear, lowered its head and pulled up the collar of its coat.

A strange weeping sound came from it and its heavy shoulders heaved convulsively.

The Hawklord stood motionlessly behind it, taken aback. Another thought occurred to him. Nervously he reached out his hand once more and rested it on the trembling shoulder.

"I'm not looking at your face, Spike. I was just glad I found you…"

But the sobbing noise grew louder and more hysterical. Finally, a muffled, panic-stricken voice came from below the lowered head. "I'm sorry, Al!" it pleaded. "I'm sorry for spoiling it! You are dead. You can't trick me…our bombs killed you." It paused, choking. ". . . I knew you'd escape and get me! I guess I've been waiting for you."

The Hawklords looked at one another in amazement.

"Take it easy," Astral Al said. "You dropped no bombs. What are you going on about?"

The mutant turned round again, more slowly this time. Its face was wet, and its eyes almost hidden in the thick holes of flesh. It looked crazed.

"The *atom bombs*! The War! We *nuked* you! Have you forgotten that? We nuked half the planet! America's the only place left and we're the only survivors…"

"He must mean in his own Time Stream, before it got forced off into the Time Faults," Thunder Rider interrupted. "He thinks we belong to his own Time. There must have been some kind of war…"

They watched the creature in front of them and listened to its rambling words. They tried to imagine the massive catastrophe that had taken place. Perhaps the nuclear war that had once threatened Mankind long ago in their own Time before other equally effective kinds of destruction had done the job, had been enacted here instead.

"What war do you mean?" Thunder Rider asked it.

"Vietnam!" the reply came back, shocking them with its implications. "You must know what happened? But you must *know* all that!" It began to laugh hysterically now, and its breathing had become heavier. "Maybe the dead forget, but I can't forget! The living must suffer!" it gasped. "The Queens…They've broken their word…they promised to keep you away from us…"

"The Red Queen?" the Light Lord started. He turned quickly to the mutant. "What do you mean, 'keep us away'? Where did the Queen say she'd kept us?"

It blinked at them through swollen rolls of flesh, now in obvious confusion. "The stadium…the Queens captured you…"

"Not us," the Light Lord told it. He turned to the Hawklords. "He may think we're Patti and the band…"

"What stadium?" Lord Rudolph now ran to the mutant and shook it. But the creature seemed to suffer a stroke.

It began sliding down the door, clawing at the garments restricting its throat. "Goodnight's coming…I've left it too late…I must…get inside…!" Feebly, it tried to turn and open the door once more, but fell helplessly to the floor, writhing.

The Hawklords felt a raising of negative energy in the irradiated air. Pressure built up inside their heads and a sensation of nausea came inside them. The air round about grew unusually cold.

"Uh, it's that music again…" Lord Rudolph choked.

In the distance they could hear the familiar roar of approaching bike engines.

The Hawklords began rocking back and forth in an attempt to dispel the unpleasant effects which were far more powerful this time.

"The key!" Thunder Rider jumped from his Starstreaker and began heaving at the shape of the mutant on the floor. Astral Al helped him and together they dragged the heavy body clear. He retrieved the key and stood up, but already the phosphorescent glow around his body was beginning to take on the sickly hue characteristic of huge doses of the Dark Music.

Sluggishly, he inserted the key in the lock and turned it. He pressed open the door and with his failing strength dragged the mutant inside, out of sight.

Lord Rudolph and the Light Lord dismounted.

They looked around for somewhere to hide the Starstreakers in the overgrown, junk-filled garden. The Light Lord pointed to the voluminous growth of privet hedge at the bottom of the garden.

"They won't be visible from the road."

He began to remount his machine, but Lord Rudolph stopped him.

"I've thought of a quicker way than that."

He closed his eyes and stood motionlessly. A furrow of deep concentration crossed his brow.

As the Light Lord watched him, the Starstreakers began to rise. Unsteadily at first, and then more smoothly, they skimmed in unison across the garden towards the hedge.

At the last moment, their power supply seemed to falter and they collided.

With a crunch of metal they fell heavily to earth.

The Light Lord cringed.

Lord Rudolph sagged visibly. "Sorry about the landing," he gasped. "The Dark Music's stronger than I thought."

Shakily, they withdrew their music guns and stumbled after the others into the house.

They staggered down a narrow passageway and came to a large wide room filled with strange shapes and forms. At the window, Thunder Rider and Astral Al were crouching down in abject misery, their music guns drawn and pointing through the glass towards the street outside.

D-RIDERS

The roar of the bikes grew louder, and the rays of Dark Music mounted in intensity.

Soon, they could hear the notes of the music itself above the noise of the engines, and their condition grew worse.

Silly Love Song.

It was the tune of a forgotten rock band that had existed sometime in the Pre-Dawn era.

They watched with rigid faces, now scarcely able to speak, trying to blot out the pounding waves of unconsciousness that beat in their skulls. Their fingers moved feverishly about their gun butts, seeking the play buttons.

"Low volume," Thunder Rider warned, gasping for breath, "or we'll give ourselves away. Point them at your heads…"

Soothing Hawkwind music began to issue faintly from the miniature loudspeakers.

They lifted their guns to their temples and pressed the nozzles against the fragile bone.

The music played almost inaudibly, discharging small bursts of extra light into the room, filling their beings with a radiant energy.

"At least that should keep us conscious," the Light Lord said. "We'll have to raise it a bit if they get any closer."

"They can't get much closer than this!" Astral Al remarked. "Here they come!"

As he spoke, a column of the motorcycle cops burst into view. This time they rode four wide and about twenty deep, sitting aloof in their seats and holding their handlebars at arms' length. They stared impassively ahead at the road through shades. On their heads, white crash helmets squashed on to their ungainly forms.

The column swept slowly, sedatedly by, occupying the width of the road. At their head rode a single, large figure — a giant amongst mutants. He was a full head and shoulders above his fellow ghouls and was approximately half as broad again across the shoulders. He wore a military uniform of some kind, decked in mirror-like squares and chains which were probably his medals. A flat, peaked hat bearing a bright insignia rested on his head. It was tilted forward, its peak jutting out belligerently in front of it. On the wheel assembly at the front of his bike was mounted a huge, double-coned speaker unit which sprayed the pop music to either side of him.

The sounds echoed emptily against the house fronts, crippling their inhabitants.

"Goodnight!" Lord Rudolph whispered.

"Eh?" Thunder Rider frowned.

"That was the name our mutant friend shouted out, wasn't it" the bass guitarist asked.

"They've all got speakers mounted on them," Astral Al noticed. "Only the others aren't so big," He adjusted the volume of his music gun to counteract an increase in the Dark Radiation.

The convoy roared smoothly by, as though it were a single co-ordinated machine. Then it disappeared out of sight, taking its virulent mix of pop music and Death Rays elsewhere.

"A calculated hierarchy of power living off the labours of others," Lord Rudolph continued, breathing more freely. "Familiar, eh? Each day one kind of people go out to work doing something for the benefit of the other kind of people. Each day, when they come home they get a dose of the controlling gratitude — just to remind them who's boss." He smiled bitterly. "If you don't behave you get put in a cage and used as entertainment for the pigs."

"Let's see what more we can get out of Spike," the Light Lord said, noticing the prone figure of the mutant. It was now perfectly motionless and seemed unconscious. It lay on a broken bed where Astral Al and Thunder Rider had pulled it.

"Don't bother." Astral Al surprised them. "Whatever that thing is, it isn't Spike any more. Besides, we don't need him now. I know the stadium. There's only one round here it could be, and that's the Kezar Stadium…"

The drummer felt a sorrow rise in him now, and he found himself wishing to leave the pathetic semblance of his former friend to its fate, unharmed.

Heeding his words, the Hawklords filed out of the sad, memory-filled house into the overgrown garden to their Starstreakers. The house had probably not changed all that much since he remembered it many years before in another time, in another, perhaps more pleasant place, where the Death Generator had still permitted men to live relatively happily together.

JOURNEY ACROSS A CRATER

Like a great, collapsed blister in the floor of the Time Zone, the Kezar Stadium appeared in front of them, barely recognizable as the arena that had once been used as a venue for Professional American Football and rock festivals.

It smoked sullenly, burning with a hundred fires that seemed to spring up from pits in its surface and from behind the broken and disused terraces. Complex machinery whirred and clanked amid the fires, manned by silent ghost shapes.

Like the other buildings in San Francisco they had seen, the stadium was being allowed to deteriorate. Except for the almost fanatical attention paid to gardening and park-keeping, no maintenance work of any kind seemed to be in operation in the old city. The Hawklords wondered how long such a system of neglect and cruelty could last.

Astonished by the Hell-like landscape, they raised their altitude in order to see it better, and they flew above it like four contrasting stars of good fortune. There seemed no point in stealth now. Eagerly they blasted out their music cannons.

They dropped altitude in unison and skimmed across the poisoned grass of Golden Gate Park. Now they could see more clearly inside the stadium, and scanned the industrious scene for sign of the characteristic Hawklord phosphorescence — for both Patti L'Horse and Lord Jefferson of Polyddor, being descended from the Hawklords, were endowed with these lordly signs of power.

As they glided over the lip of the building, several Bulls who had been patrolling the perimeter leapt from their Harley Davidsons and began taking pot-shots at them. But the bullets were harmlessly deflected by the protective force-field of Hawkwind music.

They entered undeterred and unruffled.

They could see the fires more clearly now, burning in deep vents in ground once reserved for a running track, emitting a sulphurous, pungent smoke. The zombie-like workforce attended to their tasks arduously, watched over by the ever-present Bulls.

The festering figures were uncaring and oblivious of the events and objects round about them.

"They must work a system of shifts," the Light Lord commented, rising up from the edge of one of the fires. He had been observing the work at closer quarters. "That siren we heard must denote a break in the shifts..."

The police Bulls appeared to be present in vast numbers, supervising the work and occasionally beating the workers with cudgel-like implements. They were disturbed by the passage of the Hawklords, and the one-time ordinary law men of the North American continent began to shy away from the effects of the Hawkwind tunes that were being broadcast.

Having discovered bullets to be useless they began defending themselves with their pocket tape recorders instead, and now the Hawklords gradually began to feel the effects of the retaliation.

The cumulative Dark Power of the many small transmissions tugged at their force-fields and bent them out of shape. They felt the cold daggers of the music stabbing them. They turned their kind of music higher and sped on resolutely above the bed of battle sparks that had now been produced.

They flew effortlessly above the fray, their minds in excellent form for guiding their craft. But their confidence waned as they searched most of the large stadium and found no sign of Patti or her band.

Then the faint strains of another music fell on their ears. It was scarcely audible above the sounds of their own music and the crackling of the sparks below. They heard it at all only because they seemed to be flying directly over its source.

"The cannons!" Thunder Rider shouted above the din.

They turned off their equipment. Abruptly, the Hawkwind music ceased and the Dark music struck them with full force.

It was a moment of agony, but it gave them sufficient time to identify the mysterious music they had heard.

"*Starstreaker!*" Thunder Rider yelled out, joy momentarily surmounting the pain that twisted inside him.

The song was the unmistakable composition of Patti, performed in her natural and spontaneous style. The familiar words drifted fleetingly to their tortured minds.

"We ride and glide to get our kicks,
We suck and fuck to get our licks,

In our machines we see the best,
With our unique orgasmic zest —
We fly where no one's ever been,
And open up the land of dreams…"

The accomplished backing of the Complete Orgasm Band — a band dedicated to encouraging in its following the physical function described in its name — rose in the air to greet them.

Half-dead from the battering they were receiving at the hands of the Bulls, the Hawklords began to descend into the fiery, smoking entrance to the vents where the music seemed to be coming.

"Cannons...open...fire!" Thunder Rider screamed hoarsely.

As one, the pilots of the Starstreakers turned their heavy artillery back on again and dived steeply earthward. Once more the crackling fronts of energy obliterated their vision, but soon they fell below the level of the stadium floor...into the mouth of the pit, where the Dark transmissions were unable to reach them.

BAND OF LIBERATION

The walls of the vent shone a bright silver in the light of the flames that licked up from below.

The air became unbearably foul and pungent as they descended. They lowered their machines cautiously, and eventually they reached the vent floor.

Here, the patches of fire blazed, their usual orange flames appearing as a silver hue in the strange lighting typical of the Death World. Mutants, their bloated skins glistening like carapices with sweat and reflected light, toiled painfully at their work. They collected debris that had been dropped by their workmates above and cast it into the flames with the aid of large metal calipers. A passageway lined with fire led away deeper into the earth, and the Hawklords turned toward it, following the sounds of the orgasmic rock music. At the tunnel's mouth, they hesitated, suspecting treachery, but they continued, knowing that they could not turn back now.

The music grew louder, and they glided almost eagerly down the passageway. The roof and walls were supported by glowing bands of metal erected closely together like the segments of a giant, psychedelic caterpillar. As they moved, the segments seemed to ripple in waves, and they experienced the oddly realistic sensation of being swallowed by peristalic motion.

The gullet-like passageway wound about, all the while dropping more steeply down. Eventually, it opened out into a large cavern with billowing, shining walls blinding them with its intensity. Here, the sound of the music was at its loudest, and on the undulating floor in front of them they were gradually able to discern the outlines of the rock band that they had pursued for so long. It was indeed the notorious Complete Orgasm Band, also known as The Band of Guitars because of the number of guitars and string instruments it had, known also as the Band of The New Man because of the inclination of its members to wander the wastelands of Earth seeking new life.

Their eyes became more adjusted to the glare, and with redoubled joy they identified the wild, dark-haired Patti L'Horse. The band's founder was spitting the words of her song into her microphone as though the thoughts that gave them birth were too explosive to be contained inside her.

Leaning in her arms was a narrow, silver harp which she plucked with a wild rebelliousness.

By her side stood the tall, prepossessing Lord Jefferson of Polyddor who belonged to the group because of his exceptional bottle neck on Brainphaser, the deadly Prince of Guitars.

There was also the muscular bass guitarist who was known as Hiwatt, with his incredible bass, Vesuvius. By his side stood The Laughing God, alias Terry Ollis, alias the Thunder Lord. And lastly there was the dark and sombre Steel Eye Skelter, his face partly deformed from contact with the Death Rays, universally respected for his 12-string double-necked cell mutator, Gate of The Gods.

Spell-bound, the Hawklords watched as the band changed from *Starstreaker* and went into *Last Outpost of Man* — by contrast a sad and melancholy ballad describing Civilization's decline.

But their joy was undermined by the knowledge that in the event they witnessed lay some sinister trap of the Red Queen's.

"*Now* what are we to do?" Lord Rudolph asked as they hovered uncertainly at the entrance to the gleaming cavern. "Is it too much to expect that Patti is playing of her own free will?"

"We could do with some more advice from you on the ways of women, Lord Rudolph," Thunder Rider commented dryly. He sounded disheartened. "Perhaps we would be able to anticipate the Red Queen's intentions."

"My wisdom stops at understanding them," Lord Rudolph declined the challenge.

"The best way to find out is to push on with it," the Light Lord told them, edging his Starstreaker forward. "The Queen's playing a game with us. She's admitted that herself in so many words. We're in a weak position at the moment. It's up to us to force her hand..."

"Fuck the bitch!" Astral Al shouted. He seemed intoxicated by the beating silver light which seemed to affect their nervous systems. "We've faced no worthy opposition so far! Whatever it is that makes the band play, there's nothing here to stop us from taking them back with us. If they're conditioned then we'll take them back with us by force."

There seemed very little else they could do, and they began to drift out towards the performing rock band.

The players seemed deeply involved with their music, as though only their images had been presented to the advancing Hawklords, projected as a trick.

But the theory was dispelled when Lord Jefferson of Polyddor looked up from his guitar work and noticed them. An astounded expression appeared on his face and in the glare of the light it seemed as though he grinned and waved to them. Then Patti too noticed them from her microphone. She broke her number and screamed out, delight on her face.

"DAD!"

"PATTI!" Thunder Rider shouted, unable to contain his feelings any longer.

Caught up in the euphoria of the reuniting, Lord Rudolph speeded up his craft, but too late he noticed the real look on his son's face.

The figure of Lord Polyddor was waving them *away*, and he was shouting a soundless warning at them above the din made by the music. Angrily, the figure threw down his guitar and ran to the microphone.

The music began to break up and stop as the other players realized what was happening, only now a further force acted to ensure that the gallant rescuers were unable to pull back, even had they wished to.

It was a force that tugged and tore at their cells and dissolved their minds, a force they had felt on many other less desperate occasions.

"The Time Zone Wall!" Thunder Rider yelled out. "We're flying into the wall!"

Their minds lost resistance to the force that had taken them over, and they prepared themselves grimly to be jettisoned into an unknown world. Had they wished to re-enter their own time they would have had to phase back through the wall at the point of their entry. They were now far removed from it.

THE QUEENS OF DELIRIA

The individual atoms and molecules of the Hawklords' bodies were dissociated by the impartial fingers of Time. Instead of passing through the Time Wall as they expected, their particles were seized by a machine of colossal power that processed them and restructured them and trapped them inside itself.

They came to consciousness standing on a vast ledge of some kind. They were on foot, at the edge of a deep, rocky chasm that gouged into the ground. Unlike the Death World, the day was clear and bright and there were colours. In the depths below them they could see the spray rising from a raging river glinting in the natural sunlight.

But something was wrong with Reality.

The objects they saw lacked depth and perspective, and the landscape seemed to hang vertically in front on their faces, unbearably jumbled and close. The foaming watercourse below looked close enough to lick, while a tiny pebble balanced on the chasm edge could have been mistaken for a distant mountain peak.

"Get back to the Time Zone Wall!" Astral Al shouted.

They tried to move.

They felt their bodies turning round. They watched their legs walking. They saw the scenery revolving. But they did not seem to make any progress.

The Time Wall no longer appeared to exist.

"We better stop," Thunder Rider told them. "If we keep moving about aimlessly, we could go over the edge. It's impossible to see what we're doing…"

He fought to keep down the overriding panic he felt trying to consume him.

"We seem to be in some kind of a film," the Light Lord cried. "It's two dimensional…"

Thunder Rider bent down to touch the ground in front of his feet. His hands closed on empty air and he realized with sudden shock that he was standing at the chasm edge. Now, it seemed, he could no longer tell which way his body lay in relation to the landscape.

Fighting down his fear, he closed his eyes and relied on his memory to re-orientate himself. When he opened his eyes he was relieved to notice the faces of the other Hawklords by his side. Their flat surfaces pressed on top of his vision.

Remembering the chasm edge, he stepped away from it.

"It's the Grand Canyon!" he said.

His voice sounded loud and sharp, and now the racing adrenalin inside him began to dissipate and he felt mildly drugged.

"This is some trick of the Red Queen's. Reality is exactly the same as it was, only we seem to be seeing it differently."

His words made the others feel slightly better, although their minds and bodies were still far from adapting to the new sensations.

A loud "CLICK" sounded. Simultaneously, the scenery in front of them went dark.

Momentarily they experienced total darkness, then a new scene appeared. This time they found themselves standing by Mount Rushmore, a whole mountainside carved into the massive busts of early American Presidents: Roosevelt, Lincoln, Washington, and Jefferson.

It was another early United States landmark — still presented to them in the same film-like manner.

"What reality, Thunder Rider?" Lord Rudolph asked, some of his natural irony returning despite himself.

Before anyone could reply, there was a further "CLICK." The scenery around them changed again. This time they were taken on to the windy shores of a vast sea or lake that no one could recognize.

"This sounds really weird to say," Astral Al spoke. A fatal fascination with their predicament had gripped him. "Somehow we've been trapped in a two-dimensional film. That clicking sounds like the noise a slide projector makes…"

Uncertainly, they waited for the next shift.

"CLICK!"

Without warning they were moved again, this time to a city location.

They recognized the wrought-iron balconies and the colourful buildings of the New Orleans Latin Quarter. Sightseeing buses and cars jammed the street and loudly-dressed pedestrians thronged the pavements. The scene was an exact visual creation of the city's Mardi Gras as it would have appeared towards the end of Civilization.

"CLICK!"

"CLICK!"

In quick succession they were taken on a guided tour of the major U.S. sights: — the Empire State Building, Pearl Harbour, the giant redwood forests — and many other places they were unable to recognize.

At length they found themselves standing on the lawn of the White House in Washington.

They waited for the "film" to change again, but this time it did not.

"Now what are we supposed to do?" Thunder Rider asked, perplexed. "Is this real or isn't it?" He indicated the former Presidential building.

"The door's open," Astral Al noticed. "Maybe that's a hint."

"The Red Queen's up to her tricks," Thunder Rider murmured. "I suppose we might as well try. It's better than doing nothing."

They set out across the White House lawn towards the wide doorway.

The freshly mown grassy slope stretched imperceptibly uphill. Both lawn and building seemed to belong to the same plane. It was as though they were walking towards something which had no distance.

They had to walk slowly, keeping their arms in front of them to prevent coming against the building too suddenly.

The White House doorway gradually increased in size as they drew closer. Soon they had arrived in front of it.

"Now we can at least test whether we're in a film or not," Lord Rudolph said. "If we can pass through into a new 'set', we can't possibly be in a film…"

Hardly had he uttered these words than they found themselves able to see inside the dim interior of the house.

Cautiously they stepped inside, and found themselves in a large hallway.

The scene had changed.

"Maybe this is a film, and maybe *we're* the characters in it," the Light Lord voiced their uneasy thoughts. "In which case do we exist at all?"

They stared at the trappings of Presidency that adorned the tall walls. They were unable not to look for the scene filled their visual field, and the brilliantly coloured objects in it clamoured crudely for their attention.

"There's too many...it's too much!" Astral Al protested, shielding his eyes.

"We must go further!" Thunder Rider told them. "Until we find a way out..."

They moved like blind men, sighted, yet sightless among the thousands of objects around them. They were distinguished from their surroundings by the slender thread of self-awareness that propelled them, that told them that they were Hawklords.

They moved up wide, spreading staircases and stumbled along white corridors and through palatial, sparsely furnished rooms with polished floors.

"Red Queen!" Lord Rudolph shouted out. "We know you can hear us! If this is your idea of a joke, it's a weak one."

They entered one of the President's Rooms, windowless and furnished with a single large desk. Flag posts stood proudly in holders at either side. A portrait of Washington hung on one wall.

"Nothing," said Astral Al.

They moved on, and in another passageway, came to a door marked "Blue Room."

"This is where a lot of them used to sit," Lord Rudolph commented. "In their days of power!"

They opened the door and stepped inside.

The room was painted a pale, egg-shell blue, and was a classical oval shape. Here were hung more portraits of the Presidents. This time there were seven of them, neatly and equally spaced around the room. The flooring was rich, lightly hued parquet tiling. At one end of the oval stood a suite of luxury divan armchairs. At the other was a solid, wooden desk, forming a perfect symmetrical balance. Behind the desk sat a figure, staring expressionlessly at them, and they stopped in the open doorway, transfixed by its gaze.

She was a bright, carmine red, and her surface rippled when she moved.

"Welcome at last to Deliria, Hawklords!" she crooned. "What a pity you have been so foolish to stray here, although I must admit you have had a little help!"

The figure laughed affectedly, and they were too taken aback by its presence to reply immediately.

The Red Queen seemed to wear no robes — at least her robes appeared to be a part of her skin, assuming that they existed at all. Her facial features were clear, yet oddly indistinct.

"We're not fools, Madame," Lord Rudolph replied, collecting his wits. "We've come for our children and we intend to take them. Don't think your world frightens us...you've seen what our music can do. We came here willingly, knowing the dangers."

"Then you are fools to take your lives so lightly and adding your deaths to those of your kinsfolk!" came the warmly sarcastic reply. "But now I have you I don't care whether you realized the trap or not. I admit I am disappointed that your friends decided to return to that ridiculous city of yours. I had hoped to catch you all, but that can wait. They will follow on."

"You will be sorry for speaking so lightly of my daughter," Thunder Rider warned her angrily. "It is you who is the fool, Red Queen!"

"Take seats, Hawklords! I hate to keep my guests standing!" she intoned sharply. Then her voice mellowed again and she raised an arm, indicating the suite of chairs. "Please. By the way, Lord Rudolph; referring to your comment about the Presidential seat of power just then — don't you think I make a good successor to my worthy antecedents?"

Her fluid shape twisted as she swept an arm around the room, indicating the motionless portraits.

"We'll decline your offer of hospitality," Thunder Rider told her. "We aren't bargainers. Nor do we concede defeat..."

"My dear," the Red Queen spoke patronizingly, "you are as defeated as my last presidential opponent! As for your position, how can you be so sure of it when you cannot possibly know what I have in store for you?"

"You did not dare to face us in the open...in your own land or in ours," Lord Rudolph challenged her. "You have had to trap us first."

The figure seemed to melt with affection. "My poor defeated opponents. Don't you realize I gave you fair play? Have you not forgotten the rules of democracy which enable candidates for the Presidency to state their campaigns freely without coercion? Instead of fighting you, I gave you the chance to establish your popularity with the American citizens — and some success you had with them, I must say! I have been following your adventures with a keen interest."

"Democracy! You perverted tart!" Astral Al yelled out. "You cow! There's no democracy here — only a load of bad vibrations coming from you..."

"Save your breath, drummer! You don't have long to keep it!" the Red Queen snapped. Her colour flushed a deep crimson. "Those who refuse to play in the game as you have done must be counted out."

"Then tell us, now that you have established your presidency, what you intend doing with your powers?" Lord Rudolph asked her guilefully.

Her colour reasserted its usual shade. "You're clever, Lord Rudolph...but I will tell you. There is no reason now why you should not be told as you shall not be leaving Deliria alive! My object had been to serve the Death Generator and to oppose the forces of the ancient Baasark which you Hawklords represent. You have successfully conquered our forces in your own Time. I grant your victory with a certain respect. To combat you we have had to establish the Throdmyke power here instead, in a different Time. Our campaign, I am glad to say, has met with success..." she chuckled.

"Yet it has been predicted that the Hawklords will destroy the Death Generator. Surely you must know that!" Thunder Rider interrupted.

"You are stupid to believe in fairy tales, Hawklord!"

"Mephis was a fairy tale?" the Light Lord asked amusedly. He sounded surprised. "He once tried to rule as you have done, and we destroyed him!"

"Mephis!" the voice hissed contemptuously. They felt an icy draught blow on them as the Red Queen's figure puffed itself out. "You insult me! The sacred energies of the Dark Force that ran through that man were wasted! He had no idea how to control the gifts of the Dark Ones. His meddling produced only one good thing — the war that unwittingly caused the Time Faults to appear. Thanks to that I have been brought closer to you and have been better able to launch my attack. No, Hawklords, you will be the losers this time — you and your race of do-gooders!" Once more her voice mellowed. "But I forget myself again. We Queens pride ourselves on our diplomacy..."

"We?" Thunder Rider asked.

"The Queens of Deliria!" came the proud reply. Her voice echoed shrilly round the room. "All of us! There is a Queen for each State in Deliria!"

"You mean the United States," the Light Lord corrected her.

The carmine figure pulled itself into a roughly diamond shape in evident delight. "No, my dear. I mean *Deliria*! That is the name given to my realm by my subjects, and I think it a fair one..."

"Have you not considered that your subjects have named it this from despair?"

"Of course! That is the point!" the Red Queen replied exaltedly. "Their misery makes me happy! You see," she continued confidingly, "we Ghouls thrive off misery!" She laughed at her own joke. Noticing the expression of disgust on their faces she added, a trifle more seriously: "We get a psychic kick from suffering — pain gives us our energy. Why do you think we put our subjects to toil? But I can see I am in danger of boring you..."

"Those prisoners in the cages..." Astral Al muttered to the three Hawklords by his side. "Spike, the zombies at the stadium...We must get Patti and break this place apart. We can take anyone who wants to come back with us!"

"Go easy," Lord Rudolph told him. "She is invulnerable now, or she wouldn't be so sure of herself."

The drummer gritted his teeth. It was impossible for them to move rapidly without misjudging distances and losing all sense of themselves in their two-dimensional surroundings.

He fingered his music gun, and he wondered whether it would have any effect on the Red Queen.

"Where's the Orgasm Band?" he demanded.

"Ah, of course, how forgetful of me!" the voice scolded. "Naturally you would want to know that! But haven't you met them yet?" She sounded genuinely puzzled.

"If you mean in that cavern, we have. But we've seen nothing of them since," Thunder Rider replied.

"Well, in that case, you have seen that they are safe," the Red Queen continued. "But is this of any consequence now? They are safe only as long as you are, for I have planned one fate for you all. I felt you would prefer it that way."

"Your Excellence is most considerate," Lord Rudolph told her sarcastically. "I am sure we all thank you for your little charity."

"Stop bullshitting, Lord Rudolph!" Astral Al told him hotly. "You're playing into her hands." He pulled out his music gun and pointed it at the Red Queen. "Either you take us to Patti and Lord Jefferson or I'll turn this on."

"You're so beautiful when you're angry like that, angel!" the Queen smiled lasciviously. She sighed, "Sometimes I regret not being a plain, ordinary American housewife again...but no matter. You poor child! You must be hard pressed to use your feeble weapon, and obviously have little understanding of your position!"

Angrily the Hawklord depressed the play button on his gun, but as the Queen had implied, it was dead. In frustration he played with the volume control, but the gun still would not play.

"What have you done to it?" he shouted at her.

"I have done nothing to it," the Queen replied levelly. "The gun is perfectly sound — in the right dimension! It's what I have done to you that counts!" She laughed, but then grew serious. "I must confess, I am upset about your reluctance to give me credit, Hawklords. After all, I have conceded your former victory over our powers. If you are true fighters you should concede mine." She sounded hurt. "This has been no simple campaign against you. I have planned meticulously for many centuries, though not of course in this Time Stream. I no longer speak as a mortal — that part of my being died long ago. Mounting our attack from a parallel Time Stream was a recent idea. We have known of your existence for as long as the Death Generator has been planted — as you have known of ours — and so we have had plenty of time to prepare...After out previous defeat we simply put the clocks back and started again, for as you know, the fight between us has crossed Time as well as Space..."

The Hawklords listened raptly.

A fleeting memory of their earlier incarnations as Hawklords millennia ago, came to them — the Hawklords who once roamed the grassland of a young Earth, during the first Magical Age, acting out their roles against the weapon of the Throdmyke. They knew that the Queen was appealing to them as equals in the war between Good and Evil.

"We cannot recognize your power," Thunder Rider told her at last. "We are not like you. To us, this war means much more than a game. Deep down, you must know this for you've taken the form, and therefore the minds, of many mortals and must know what thing it is you are perverting..."

"No! No!" the Red Queen cried. "I don't know that! You are making the premise that life is basically good. We both know that this is not so." Her guard rose once more. There was definite malice in her voice. "But as you wish. You say you cannot concede my victory. What you are really saying is that you consider yourselves above me, that it is I who should belittle myself to you! Very well, I shall spell out your position, and you will see how hopeless I've made it for you and your kind!"

As she spoke, she became crimson again.

She pulsed brilliantly; her folds, that might have been garments, undulated hypnotically in front of them.

Abruptly she vanished from among the clutter of objects in their vision. "CLICK!"

Again the scene went blank.

THE LIES OF WATERGATE

White dots and streaks appeared briefly in the blackness around the four waiting Hawklords, reminding them of blank film footage running through a projector. Then a new scene burst explosively out at them. As before, it seemed to occupy a single plane. This time it depicted a picture of death and destruction.

They stared out at the gaunt, skeletal shells of buildings.

In the background a thick, black column of smoke poured up into the sky.

"Earth City!" the Light Lord gasped. "It can't be..." They gazed aghast as they recognized the domed shapes of the buckled superstructures. The outer skins of the buildings had melted and burnt away, covering the streets with solidified rivers of a lava-like substance.

"The bastard!" Astral Al screamed out. He struggled forward, but was unable to move.

This time, the picture that trapped them did not seem to be a part of *them*, although *they* still seemed to be a part of it. He beat on the surface in front of him. Although he met with no resistance, he made no progress either.

The scene changed again, and this time they saw a closeup of one of the streets — which one they could not say, for it had been so badly altered. In the shapeless substance that had dripped off the burning buildings and then cooled, they saw with horror the limbs and bodies of the Children, stuck to the ground as though they had been stage puppets and not human beings.

"Murderess!" Thunder Rider shouted. "What have you done to them?" A feeling of blind rage combined with numbing despair at the sight of the hard-won fruits of their labours — callously reduced once more to nought — consumed him. He felt the frustration of their helpless position lock his limbs in a paralysis.

They watched willingly, yet unwillingly, their eyes drawn as in a dream to the drama, observing the extent of the butchery.

The scenes changed in quick succession, revealing that little, if any, of Earth City remained. Only the stage and the hill top appeared to have survived the fire, although these had suffered apparently mindless damage from some unknown agency.

Still they were prevented from moving further into the scenes by an invisible power that held them captive.

"It would be pointless to move, even if you could," the Red Queen's cold voice came over to them. "You forget that your precious city is in another Time, and is no more accessible to you now than Life itself!"

"Have you done *this*?" Lord Rudolph asked, rigid with suppressed emotions. "If you have, there will be no place small enough for you to hide when we are free!"

The voice sounded contemptuous. "So you still talk as though your fate is not sealed! I cannot understand you. But yes, my servants, my allies in your own Time have destroyed your city. I have tried to tell you once already that you have failed."

"I did not think you would do this…" Thunder Rider spoke in a voice scarcely above a whisper. "The Children, they could have done you no harm…"

"Your mission is over," their captoress continued, ignoring him. "The whole world must be ours. We cannot leave anything alive. You have been fools. While you have spent your time rebuilding the society that Mephis so nearly destroyed, I have been busy planning your *complete* destruction. Do not think that I have not been thorough, for I have had all of Time. Ironically for you, I began the main part of my plan in your own age — the part you call the Pre-Dawn Era. I needed power to live…I needed people. Your enlightened, though confused age contained the kind of people who would sacrifice themselves to me…my subordinates, the future Queens of Deliria." She laughed. Her voice had lost its anger. Now it carried the tones of one awed by the glory of their own idealism, and convinced by it. She spoke from her invisible position somewhere off-film, as more scenes of the destruction changed in rapid succession before the gaze of the Hawklords.

"It was an age in which the Baasarkian influences were gradually rising, and my own — the Throdmyke power of the Death Generator — was waning. You were throwing off the chains of our control with mystic gurus, rock bands and consciousness altering drugs and building new societies of your own. But I caught you at a stage of confusion, as well as growth. You were so set on doing your thing, so keen to rebel against us, and so blinded by what was new, you let down all your controls and guards. You over-indulged...Of course you had a few notable successes, you stopped the Vietnam War, and you exposed the scandals of Watergate. These were two of our key attacks against you, to reassert our power. It hurt...With the power of the Death Generator I put the next stage of my plan into action. This was to isolate myself and my converts from your age so that we could build up our attack against you without disturbance. It seemed a good idea to split ourselves off before the issues of Watergate and the Vietnam War had been won by you, as we would then have a means of control in the new Time Stream...in Deliria. Originally Deliria was an entire alternative Earth system. We had managed a full conversion without most of the inhabitants realizing it..."

As she spoke, the scenes changed again, this time to locations in the past which were obviously intended to illustrate her words:

The long halls of the White House...with groups of human figures standing in heated conversation outside open doors...the Blue Room with a confident President Nixon and aides in lazy conference, dropping expletives and the names of "enemies"...packed court rooms...newspaper headlines...the smiling face of the President talking to the world on the television, lies fixed in the misty glassiness of his eyes...a jungle village in Indo-China showing burning huts and fleeing families clutching children...a group of solemn grey-suited figures (one of them a woman of striking beauty) in extensive laboratories...the group performing a ritual ceremony while white-coated scientists operated complex apparatus. The silent figures seemed somehow to be tapping the power of the machine, as though guiding it along mysterious channels, acquiring the magic necessary to create the new Time Stream of Deliria.

"We made sure that in Deliria the Watergate Tapes were not found," the voice continued, "and retained our control — just as we also ensured that the war with the Communists was not resolved...!"

In quick succession came newsreel scenes of the atrocities; the police and armed forces of many different countries around the world shooting and clubbing rioting civilians...wholesale slaughter of hippies massed together in camps that looked like outdoor music festivals...soldiers battling and tanks bursting through buildings...the smiling face of the President taken with the same beautiful lady...shot of the H-bomb exploding, the dust enlarging, billowing out and growing, swelling into its infamous fungoid shape...

From the devastation came the Red Queen's unremitting and unrepentant voice. "Then, as you know, a part of our land was ripped away in the Time Quakes. This had the effect of splitting us up and dividing our power — but also it brought us closer to you. By chance, the Time Fault proved an ingenious aid and would have saved us much time had I thought of it to begin with!

"Now I come to the part of the story which concerns you directly. It will answer the questions that you have been too proud to ask! You were right, Light Lord, about the medium you have been trapped inside — it is very much like a film..." She laughed self-consciously. "To regain our lost empire, my scientists had to devise a machine that would reclaim it and the ruling Queens stranded on it, and bring them through the Time Fault. We had to transport Deliria here! The process of recreation we have used takes place in two stages. Firstly the machine, which we call a Transmogrifier, absorbs and stores the object to be transported in a two-dimensional form. This it does on a special computer tape. In the second and final stage it restores the "film" holographically back into three dimensions. So far we have only managed to recreate isolated areas of our former world. We have managed to increase the size of San Francisco, but we've got most of the United States inside the memory banks, as you saw on the first film I showed you. It will only be a question of time before our main seat of power will be recreated in 3-D, and my co-monarchs will be able to join me again in their rightful positions..." The Red Queen sounded bitterly triumphant, as though she foresaw the righting of a thousand injustices which had been done to her during her existence. The landscape around the Hawklords had turned into a swirl of meaningless, abstract colours and patterns.

"It is you, then who is responsible for the Displacement Effects..." Thunder Rider stated rather than asked, remembering the incongruous objects that had appeared in the deserts outside Earth City, and in the City itself.

A shocked look appeared on his face.

"The Time Zone...we saw it growing...! You can't recreate it all here! You'll destroy the entire planet...!"

The monarch laughed harshly. "An unexpected bonus on our part! As you see, there is no hope for you at all! If by the remotest chance you evade the fate I have lined up for you here, as you insist you will, you will be returned to a world who's days are numbered, and all in it shall perish...!"

"But what of the Displacement Effect?" the Light Lord asked, staggered by the enormity of the deathly operation the Red Queen had described. "Where will the planet go to? It won't just cease to exist! The Time Laws of Displacement state that it will go into the intruding Time-Stream...into Deliria. Your project will be self-defeating."

"No!" she shrilled. "The Time Laws state that displaced matter is dispersed at random throughout Time and Space! Any that finds its way into Deliria will be automatically absorbed by the Transmogrifier and ejected outside our Time boundaries."

"You will destroy the fabric of Time itself then!" Lord Rudolph declared, horrified. "You cannot undermine the Time Worlds by bringing one into another without risking the collapse of the whole."

"That I concede to be true, but what can I do now?" the Queen told him. "I must take that risk! We cannot go backwards...we must consolidate ourselves or I risk the far worse fate of finding my subjects in a limbo, with nowhere to go."

"You have gambled foolishly with both Life and the Universe," Lord Rudolph told her savagely. "With things that did not belong to you!"

"Don't anger me Hawklord, or I shorten your remaining time! I am sure you wish to know how you have been deceived before you die..."

"You have an overriding wish to tell us, that is plain!" Thunder Rider said to her archly. "I am not a Ghoul like you! I have no wish to know!"

"Liar!" she screamed. "I understand you better than you understand yourself, and you will be told!"

"It seems we have no choice," Astral Al sneered.

'Silence!" the voice shrieked. Abruptly, her mood changed again, for her voice became level once more. "I forget my position," she told them quietly. "I must remind you...I need the life energy of *people* in order to survive. You *small* band are Hawklords...and *your* Life Energy is greater than all mortals put together. With it I can rule the Universe. It will pass to me on you death, and I cannot afford to miss the opportunity of acquiring it. Even your present suffering is giving me greater strength than I had dreamed, and that is why I have to make sure you know all the painful details. For the more anguish you suffer, the more I will benefit. Now do you understand me? It is not from vanity or sadism as you seem to think, that I desire to tell you..."

The Hawklords listened to her with more abhorrence and loathing than they were able to express. Despite her words they were unable to prevent themselves feeling an unknown dread and fear — which began to feed her being.

"You're obscene!" the Light Lord managed to tell her. "You are fouler than I had ever imagined, and I take back nothing I have said against you!"

"That pains me greatly!" she mocked. "Save your words, for they will not save *you*! When I lured you here by kidnapping your offspring you became trapped not only inside Deliria, but in the machine that created it!" she cried. "To obtain energy the Transmogrifier has to be plugged into the Time Zone Wall. You entered its field of influence when I tricked you into flying at this part of the Time Zone Wall...Now your bodies are stored inside it. But don't think for one moment that it will be resurrecting you!"

"But we heard Patti's music..." Thunder Rider began, unable to help responding to the inexorable words of this parasitic being.

"Your children and their idiotic band were a mere projection of the Transmogrifier's. They were able to see you and you were able to see them, but they did not exist at that point in Space. Their music is too dangerous to play in Deliria."

"Then where are they?" Astral Al demanded. "You told us they were OK."

"And they are…yet," the Red Queen replied. "We still keep their projection at the stadium to demonstrate the extent of our power over our enemies — it keeps the mutants in check! But you will be meeting them at any moment and you can see for yourself, for there is nothing left to tell you now. I have shown you the hopelessness of your position. Whichever way you turn you will lose! And now my body grows impatient for the greater power it is soon to receive from you…."

She moaned, and the aimless, swirling colours about the Hawklords turned into blackness once more. The machine that held them in its memory "CLICKED" madly, and they felt themselves being moved about from place to place once more, though now the scenery was invisible.

"Ahhh!" the Red Queen's voice gasped with sudden pleasure, "You must die! Now! You…will…see…what…enjoyment…I…have…devised…for…myself…"

DESCENDING REDNESS

The Hawklords found themselves on a vast, yellow plain.

Blurred, indistinguishable shapes, red, greens and blues, towered on the horizon. They noticed with relief that perspective and colour had been returned. At least it had returned to their perceptions. They were able to see into the distance and move assuredly on their feet again.

"Now what?" the Light Lord asked nervously. They looked around them at the perfectly still, meaningless scene, wondering from where the next attack was to come.

"It looks artificial," Thunder Rider noticed, staring around him. "There's no proper sky…"

They looked up at a pale, rust-red ceiling, where strange amorphous shapes moved deep in its haze.

"Whatever she does to us, there must be a way of combatting her," Thunder Rider continued, racking his brains to work out the nature of their surroundings. They seemed out of focus, yet nigglingly familiar. "She's obviously mad as a hatter."

"Not as loopy as Mephis," Astral Al commented. He began walking towards one of the distant shapes. "Don't wait there to be attacked."

But he didn't get far away before he noticed figures walking towards him. He stopped and frowned, then grinned.

"Patti...Lord Rudolph!" He turned to the others. "It's the band. They're OK!"

He ran forward to greet them, but as the Orgasm Band drew closer, bearing their instruments on their shoulders, they looked pale and haggard, and they did not smile. Only the Laughing God seemed at all collected. Thunder Rider and Lord Rudolph ran forward and embraced their large children.

"It's good to see you, Dad" Lord Polyddor spoke into his father's hair, and meant it. "But it's no use getting happy about it. She let us take our instruments...as a gesture."

"What are you talking about?" his distressed father cried. "You act as though we were going to die!"

"We are!" Patti broke from Thunder Rider's agonized clasp and turned wildly towards Lord Rudolph. "You must know that whore's powers!" She waved her arms scornfully about her. "This is our Dying Ground!" She hugged her father again and cried, "You shouldn't have followed, Dad."

Thunder Rider broke free and stared accusingly at them. "You've been brain-washed if you believe that! You must believe you are going to *Live*, otherwise you're giving her the biggest weapon to use against us...!" He gazed challengingly at each member of the Orgasm Band in turn. In many ways they were still children. The band did not respond. They stared gloomily at the yellow floor .

"It's touching to see your paternal instincts coming out, Hawklords," a drowsy female voice sounded suddenly from above them. "I had children myself once. It will be most interesting to see whether they take heed of your sound advice..."

The Hawklords looked quickly up.

The reddish-brown sky had disappeared, and the moving shapes that swam in it could now be seen clearly. They were the rippling features of the Red Queen — only now she had become massive, a mountainous mass leaning over them.

"I have been generous, haven't I?" she asked anxiously. "To allow the family reunions..." She grew urgent. "But I can give no more favours. You must give them to me instead...and play for me!"

As though resolved by a camera lens, the blurred shapes round about leapt into focus.

"When the ball hits you, your patterns preserved in the Transmogrifier shall be erased!" she told them. "Then, only a few Hawklords and a razed city will stand between me and Earth!"

The overloaded senses of the Hawklords refused at first to recognize the colossal, spring-like bumpers capped with shining steel, and the vivid, elongated lettering painted on the ground.

Then Steel Eye Skelter laughed a scornful, black-hearted laugh. "Pin-ball!"

He turned his deformed face towards Thunder Rider and pointed at his scars. "I got these fighting Mephis — I'm not about to give up now!"

He flung back his head and screamed at the Red Queen.

"Hear that, you old shag bag?"

His voice was drowned by a loud rumbling.

The giant pin-table shook with sudden force, and they realized that the game was underway.

The shaking grew worse as the roar of the steel ball rolling in the distance at the top of the table drew closer. Neck-jolting crashes came as the solid steel sphere started careering into the bumpers and bashing against the sides of the table.

Despite the immense physical strength that the Hawklords possessed, they were thrown helplessly off their feet, their miniaturized bodies unable to fight against such overwhelming odds.

Fleetingly, Thunder Rider noticed that the shiny, yellow floor was gently sloping towards them and that they were gradually sliding downhill.

They were falling down inside the two large, funnel-shaped guides at the base. The guides were lined with long, belt-like rubber cushions that would deflect anything that touched them. At the base of the funnel were the two flippers, already moving in anticipation. The Red Queen would operate these to prevent the ball being lost. Beyond them was the gaping black hole where the lost ball would go. Unless they could manage to escape from the funnel before the ball reached them they would stand little chance of survival.

"Hold hands!" Thunder Rider shouted, scarcely audible above the roaring of the ball and the clattering of the huge score board above their heads.

The board was decorated with huge dice and playing cards. Numbers flashed up on its illuminated panel in rapid succession. By its side hovered the shape of the Red Queen's head, her streaks and swirls racing wildly about on the surface of her face. She seemed the pictured essence of wanton depravity.

Groggily, the Hawklords and their children searched for one another's hands and they formed a human chain. They staggered to their feet, holding one another up.

Heeding the intermittent instructions of the red-haired saxophonist, they spread out in a line and slowly made their way up the quaking slope.

Now they could see the massive bumpers with their rubber deflection cushions standing forbiddingly in front of them, and the huge silver ball, far larger than themselves bouncing about from bumper to bumper.

"We must get to the top of the table," Thunder Rider shouted. "We can shelter in the overhang where the ball shoots out!"

They advanced slowly, slipping and sliding, helping one another to remain upright. The seriffed bases of tall letters appeared on the floor in front of them—

BONUS HOLE SCORES 1,000 + 1 BONUS ADVANCE FOR EACH LIT CARD

Beyond the painted words they could see the mouth of the score hole, as wide as the Hawklords were tall. Further still, beyond the hole, was the first row of the giant bumpers.

More lettering appeared—

SPECIAL WHEN LIT
TARGETS ADVANCE — BONUS WHEN LIT
DOUBLE BONUS WHEN LIT

Lights flashed and colours popped out at them, demanding attention they were unable to give. "We'll have to split up to get past the bumpers…" Lord Jefferson gasped.

As he spoke, the steel ball shot down a narrow channel to their left, sending a flipper revolving at high velocity.

FLIPPER REVOLVING AT 20 TIMES — 20,000

The pin-table shook violently as the mechanism inside it laboured to add up the score.

The huge ball rolled in a diagonal line towards them, and except for the low rumbling sound it made, the table went quiet.

Its spheroid shape was as large as a house.

Its fluid surface reflecting the colours and shapes of the objects around it, looked harmless.

"Let go of me, you stupid bleeder!" Astral Al shouted at the Light Lord, who was gripping his hand, entranced by the sight.

He yanked his arm free and flung himself aside just in time to let the ball pass through their human chain.

It rolled rapidly by and crashed into the side of the table. Below them, from the funnel, they heard the sound of the flippers as the Red Queen desperately tried to save the deflected ball, and from above they heard her sighs of uncontrolled pleasure at the of fear they released.

A thunderous hammering sound came from the funnel and they looked back over their shoulders. The rubber deflectors had trapped the ball once more. They shot the ball backward and forward at high velocity.

As they watched, the ball broke free and came at them again; more slowly this time, up the gradient of the table.

Once more they broke to let it pass. Then, abruptly it hit the bumpers and zig-zagged back at them. It bobbed for a few seconds in the Bonus Hole, causing the lights to flash wildly. The score escalated to 5,000,000. Then it rolled sedately through them, dropping in a straight line down the table.

It fell between the gnashing flippers into the *lost* hole.

"Now's our chance to get to the top of the table!" Thunder Rider cried out. "Before she gets another ball up."

They broke up into twos and ran uphill. But the table floor was too vast for them to traverse quickly enough, and they found themselves halfway along amid the bumpers when another jolt told them that the second ball had been fired.

"Make for the right-hand wall!" someone shouted out.

They heard the smooth rumbling of the ball as it shot up the firing passageway at the side of the table.

They heard it cross the top of the table, and they did what they were bid. They lined themselves in single file along the wall, holding hands. The ball crashed into the buffer and shot explosively downward into the terminals. As it bounded back and forth, they began inching their way up the table, unable to grip the smooth wall adequately. They prayed that the ball would not suddenly be deflected their way.

They heard it clatter down into the lower half of the table, beyond the bumpers. Then it soared upward again, impelled by a flipper.

"Watch out!" the Light Lord yelled. He released Lord Rudolph's hand and they separated in time as the ball collided against the wall. The shock threw them off their feet. A resounding clang told them that the ball had rebounded against one of the bumpers.

"It's coming back!" Patti screamed, struggling to evade the monster sphere.

It smashed into the wall again, and bounded back to the same bumper.

Again it came at them, forcing them to split up and scatter. They fell, sliding and tumbling, vainly clawing at the smooth surface for support.

The shining ball changed direction, shooting abruptly upward. It hit the top of the table and then bounced back, rumbling smoothly towards where they lay.

"I...I CAN'T MOVE! HELP ME!" Patti screamed in terror.

Thunder Rider heard her cry. Wildly, he brought himself to his feet.

He summoned all the mighty Hawklord strength his body possessed, and began stumbling towards her. His speeding metabolism caused the huge death ball to appear almost stilled, but he had slipped some distance away from his daughter. Between him and Patti lay the other Hawklords, several of whom were now rising to their feet, heeding her cries.

The ball rolled towards its first victim, and Thunder Rider saw with untold anguish in his heart, that he would not be in time.

Then, Steel Eye Skelter, closer to Patti than the others, rose to his feet.

His tall, severely scarred figure floundered about, regaining its balance. It launched itself at the girl, pushing her clear of the path of the ball.

The young guitarist struggled desperately to his feet, but now the ball was on him. Instead of trying to jump clear, he sprang defiantly up at its gleaming surface, perhaps realizing that there was now no other course of action to be taken.

"NO! NO! NO! NO! NO! NO!" Patti screamed, shaking her head back and forth where she lay.

Helplessly she watched the scene. She reached up vainly to stop the heroic figure.

The airy surface of the ball swept by, taking Steel Eye with it. In horror the Hawklords watched as his body was bent by its curvature and then flattened beneath it, then sent skidding, crumpled and broken down the yellow table.

Impulsively, Lord Jefferson made as though to go after the figure, but Lord Rudolph pulled him back.

"It's no use," he said weakly.

Unable, for their own safety, to attempt collecting the body, the Hawklords formed themselves into a chain again. Bitterly, they began once more to climb up the trembling slope.

Now the ball, its damage done, was clattering about harmlessly behind them, trapped again in the funnel. From above they thought they heard the mocking laughter of the Red Queen.

They moved less confidently uphill and eventually reached the top of the firing track where its wall curved round, following the arched shape of the table. They waited in its lee.

"There must be a way out," Astral Al shouted above the roar of the ball and the clanging of the bell. "We can't sit around and die!"

He looked about him.

"We could block off the track where the balls come out," Thunder Rider suggested.

"What with?" the Light Lord asked him miserably. "Even if we did she'd free it...all we'd do is protract her pleasure by giving her more of our fear."

"Maybe," said the Laughing God, "We shouldn't be afraid. Then..."

"Then...what?" Thunder Rider asked the cryptic golden-haired drummer intently.

The Laughing God shrugged. "Who knows. . . maybe she might lose her powers."

The ball shot upward into their area and began clattering amongst the bumpers.

They watched the lights flashing, illuminating the letters.

BUTTON ADVANCE BONUS WHEN LIT
SPECIAL WHEN LIT

"Maybe," said Thunder Rider, "we believe too deeply in what we see. If this is only a film, how can an image die? What would happen if we refused to believe...?"

"We'd probably get rubbed off the tape, or whatever it is that's storing our particles!" Lord Rudolph replied.

"Not necessarily," the Light Lord pointed out. "The Red Queen told us that the Transmogrifier works by reducing and storing 3-D objects, and then reconstituting them again. Theoretically, that would mean that we were still recreatable. If we proved to be difficult objects for the machine to cope with, it might eject us instead..."

"*Eject* us?" Thunder Rider asked skeptically.

"Well, we've got minds of our own, haven't we?" Morthan Hiawatt interrupted. "We can think, we can talk...that proves we must be more than mere film images. If we refused to believe in the Transmogrifier's creations, it would *have* to eject us!"

"Not necessarily," Thunder Rider replied, still uncertain. "But if it did, where would it eject us to?"

"Who cares where it will send us to?" Astral Al asked. "Anywhere's better than here!"

"But how would we show the machine that we disbelieve it?" Lord Rudolph asked. "We couldn't just say it to ourselves...it looks too bloody real to me," he added, looking down at the zig-zagging ball.

"We'd have to do something positive that would make *us* disbelieve first, like...we'd have to act as though we really believed the ball was harmless," Astral Al said.

"You're crazy...that'd be suicide!" Patti stared at him incredulously. "Look at what it did to Steel Eye..."

"That's because he believed," Astral Al told her.

The ball shot towards them, and they parted.

It smacked thunderously against the wall behind them and bounced back again into the terminals.

"How are we going to disbelieve that?" Lord Rudolph asked, shuddering at the prospect of standing in its path.

They were silent, wishing that they were somewhere far away.

Thunder Rider stared adamantly down at the steel ball. "If we carry on as we have been doing, we die..."

As he spoke, a series of violent buffetings rocked the table.

They were accompanied by a series of crashing sounds that reverberated deafeningly through the air.

From above, came an impatient shout.

"Move, will you?"

They looked up and saw the carmine shape of their giant captoress. She was looking murderously down at them, her colours swirling agitatedly.

"She's rocking the table!" the Light Lord shouted.

They began sliding away from their hard gained position, reeling under the hefty blows that the Red Queen was delivering to the side of the pin-table.

Such was the power of the blows, they were unable to regain their footing even though they kept themselves linked together. Grimly holding one another, they were forced down again amongst the bumpers. The thumping stopped.

They climbed to their feet.

"She must have lost the ball," Astral Al commented, looking around him.

A loud crash came, followed by an ominous rumbling.

"She's fired another," Thunder Rider said, wincing already. He looked around the ring of Hawklords.

"Well, what's it to be?"

The pin ball burst out of its channel, and began dropping.

"Put plan Disbelief into action!" the Laughing God cried, smiling goldenly. He said it with such conviction that everyone instinctively nodded in agreement.

Grimly, they drew closer together and formed a tight group, In any case, they had nothing to lose. Holding hands, they waited.

The ball hit a bumper and ricocheted off.

It zig-zagged about.

Then, it cut a diagonal course towards them.

LOVE TUNNEL

A loud explosion sounded in their ears. Pain ripped at their bodies. Brilliant colours erupted in the blackness of impact. They felt their bodies bending and their bones almost snapping, but they clung resolutely to the belief that the steel ball was unable to harm them.

Those who didn't or couldn't believe this were kept from disintegrating by the strength of the others in the biological chain of energy that had been formed.

After the turbulence died down, they found themselves in a large, moist room with beating walls.

The soft floor ran with silver fluid, and steamed foully.

"It's the cavern where we saw you playing!" Lord Rudolph exclaimed to his son.

They were lying in a jumbled heap of bodies and guitars on the floor.

"The Starstreakers! They're still here!"

Groggily, the two rock bands separated themselves and climbed to their feet. They noticed the Death Radiation once more. It had increased its intensity.

The air stirred suddenly above their heads and an icy wind began moving in the warmth about them.

"Very clever, Hawklords!" a parrot-like screech of rage shrilled, hurting their ears. "But you won't get far."

"The Red Queen!" Astral Al shouted. "Let's get out of here!"

The four older Hawklords ran to their Starstreakers and climbed into their seats. The wind rose to a howling gale, frenziedly rushing about in the small enclosure.

"Climb on our knees!" Lord Rudolph shouted at Patti and her band. "You'll have to help drive them."

Lord Jefferson slung his guitar across the back of the Starstreaker and climbed on his father's knee. He gripped the bar in front of him as the machine creaked under the double load.

Patti loaded herself on Thunder Rider's lap and Astral Al and the Light Lord took Morthan Hiwatt and the Laughing God.

"Keep away from the Time Wall!" the Light Lord warned them as they slowly manoeuvred their straining craft towards the narrow opening in the cavern wall.

Thunder Rider and Patti set out first, and they squeezed through the opening into the silver passageway beyond. Behind them, the stomach walls began to convulse, and the opening began to constrict tightly, sealing the others off.

Alarmed, Thunder Rider stopped. "Turn on the music cannons!" he yelled, hoping that they would hear him.

A sudden, violent motion inside the passageway told him that they hadn't needed his advice. The sphincter-like hole expanded suddenly, and Hawkwind music burst through. A loud, animal shriek of pain echoed round the subterranean workings.

Keeping cannons trained on the pulsing rim of the opening, the other three machines worked their way through. Soon they were all inside the passageway and traveling upward.

The wind increased, blowing foully down on them.

They fought against its pressure and against the rippling silver walls of the passageway which was trying to swallow them.

Their music continued blasting out, striking at the sides with great, jagged sparks that burnt and melted the silver segments.

They reached the head of the tunnel and emerged into the fiery bed of the vent. The obnoxious smell of decaying tissue was now replaced with the sharp, choking fumes of sulphur dioxide and they hurriedly rose upward through the smoke and heat.

They turned their cannons up to full power as they came level with the stadium surface, but the display of music power which greeted them on their arrival had gone. The Work area had returned to normal. The Bulls stood casually about, goading the mutants and keeping them at the degrading tasks.

"Evidently the Red Queen's not had a chance to organize resistance," the Light Lord said, looking around from his cramped position behind the shoulders of the Laughing God.

"Well they've noticed us now!" Astral Al shouted above the noise of the music. Attracted by the sound, the mutant police were put on their guard.

The police began stumbling about, covering their ears, and some of them managed to grab their tape recorders.

Soon the whole hellish arena was ablaze again with the electrical battle sparks.

"Rise up!" Thunder Rider screamed above the noise.

Laboriously, they rose and flew upward above the fury.

They rose into the tingling bluish plasma that passed for air, and soon the strains of the Dark Music were unable to reach them. Their own Delatronized Hawkwind sound, though now inaudible to the Bulls, continued to make its presence felt to their enemies as its invisible emanations spread out over the land.

High above the stadium they stopped and held their blazing craft steady.

Then, shining more fiercely still, they streaked away towards the coast to find the Time Wall's entrance back into their own world.

BOOK THREE

MUSIC PLANET

SILT OF TIME

The once crowded surface of Earth had become waste and desert. Its civilization had gone. The remains of the people and things that had existed had been vapourized on the winds or turned to glass and eroded into powder - a fine sand that covered everywhere with a pure, cleansing mantle of whiteness.

But slowly, Earth had become silted again, this time with the lives and artifacts of all past life that had ever existed.

Shops, railways, buses, ocean liners, dinosaurs, Indians, elephants, cave men, pyramids, factories…all lay jumbled incongruously together on the sand, brought there in confusion and pain by the displacement effects of the Transmogrifier.

The partly-formed, truncated bodies of serpents threshed around in agony amongst the grisliness.

Men wandered around clutching bloodied stumps, their limbs torn savagely from them when they had been snatched through the Time Barriers. Parts of buildings had been materialized at random, forming hybrid architectural styles that conflicted with one another.

The creatures and things that had existed by virtue of their separateness had been lumped together by a cruel and careless power.

The strange layer of objects heaved and rippled, constantly changing as its components were displaced.

The Time Barriers had become fluid and meaningless, and Earth, throughout all her ages except one — the Age of Deliria — became unstable.

The Death World had begun in the Hawklords' own Time Stream.

It had become an offshoot of it. It struggled now to fulfil its vampirish aim of projecting itself back into its parent Time, and bring death to all life except its own.

Amidst the grotesque side-effects its planet-sized mass gradually appeared. The parent Zone swelled to enormous proportions. Its bulk formed an immense curtain of Darkness that rose in the sky, clearly visible from the hill top site of Earth City.

Elsewhere, Deliria materialized unevenly in a rash of Zones which covered the planet like a plague.

Their thin, cancerous stalks hung from the blue sky and their roots bit deeply into the Earth's crust.

Hourly they grew fatter and slowly merged, forming huge banks of sickly-grey mist which blotted out the sun.

MUSIC PLANET

Master and Beast stared out from Parliament Hill — the one mournful at what he saw, the other impatient for flight.

The Beast did not care much for mundane matters, and it shook its leathery wings. It nodded its horned head aggressively and dug deeply into the ground with its clawed feet.

"Easy, Leprus," the Hound Master cautioned his companion. He scratched it soothingly under his chin. "It's not so simple as you think any more. We can't just go charging off. But don't worry, I'm not leaving you behind this time."

He stared bitterly at the stricken landscapes.

For the moment, Earth City seemed to have escaped most of the displacement effects. The Time Zones too were reluctant to form over the hill top because of the Hawkwind music which was now playing again.

But Earth City had suffered badly enough.

It lay devastated from the first wave of the fighting. The hill top where the survivors had been forced to gather was all that remained.

The wild sounds of *The Aubergine That Ate Rangoon* burst intermittently from the damaged music system on the stage behind the Hawklord. The sound system crackled and rumbled, limping along; still sufficiently powerful to hold back the forces of the Transmogrifier.

The power of the Hawkwind music alone, he realized, would soon be unable to hold back the rising tide. Ultimately, the nature of the ancient power of the Baasark, which guided them in their quest to fulfil the Hawkwind Legend both produced their music...and rose above it. They were having to look to their wits.

"Come on, boy," he spoke to the winged creature again. "Back to see how work's progressing."

He turned and tugged gently at the creature's reins. But it defiantly remained where it was.

Hound Master shrugged his shoulders.

"OK, do what you want," he said disinterestedly.

He let the reins fall and started walking back towards the stage. He knew that the animal would not fly away of its own accord, no matter how strong its urge. The bond between them was too great.

"Where've you been to?" the Baron asked the Hound Master when he returned. He looked up from where he and the Boss sat in a sea of electrical parts and wires. They were repairing one of the huge stage amplifiers which had been broken in the rioting. Behind them was a large pile of other broken and smashed equipment some of it salvageable, some of it fit only for cannibalization. "We're nearly finished here," the Baron added. He indicated the stage where the tall figure of the Light Lord was visible, adding the finishing touches to a tape recording. While the Light Lord recorded, the others busied themselves checking over the musical weaponry and transport. This was no ordinary tape recording; on it depended their entire campaign to defeat the Queens — a musical bomb, comprising a collection of Hawkwind's most potent numbers. With it they planned to invade Deliria and somewhere inside, start to gig live. Under the cover that their music would afford them they hoped to feed the "wild" tape into the Transmogrifier, and wreck it.

"Some of us don't need fancy machines to ride about on!" Hound Master retorted. "Leprus doesn't need overhauling. He needs exercise and companionship instead."

"You're not coming with us on that thing!" the Crystal Princess complained. She looked up, alarmed, from where she sat grinding dried creepers in a mortar. The creepers came from the rocky plateau to the west. When their chemicals were extracted they formed a potent drug. They acted in whatever manner the user wished — as a stimulant, as an hallucinogen, as a powerful sedative to kill pain. Hurriedly the Princess poured the contents of the mortar into a jug of water, and stirred. Then she rose to her feet, carrying the jug. "I can't see what you see in him," she continued. "What are you going to do about weapons?"

"I'm not changing my mind," Hound Master stated firmly. "I promised Leprus we'd stick together. You don't know how strong he is. The Rays don't affect him."

The Crystal Princess pulled a face. "You're nuts!" she said. She turned away and walked towards where the sick Children were lying.

Dejectedly, the drummer watched her go. He felt an overriding sense of loyalty to his steed. It was a feeling that he found hard to explain. Helplessly, he looked around him for support from the band, but he got none. He decided to follow the Princess.

On his way he passed the gaping doors of the Time Vault where their equipment had been stored. The guitars and other instruments had been removed and loaded on to the Starstreakers. Miraculously they were intact, probably because of the legendary swordsman sorcerer, who, in his misery, unwittingly guarded them.

Elric had sat silently throughout the troubles, preferring the dark where he could reflect moodily on his predicament. To begin with, the Hawklords had felt hostile towards him. His desire to meet them had vanished when they had confronted him at last, and he lapsed into a deep state of despair.

He stood taller than the Hawklords, and broader. He was unaffected by either the Hawkwind music or the Death Rays, and had caused them a considerable amount of trouble. They had explained to him as best they could what had happened to him. The Earth Scientists had treated his mind to rid it of the ghosts that had possessed him, and he had seemed relieved. He had grown angry at the forces which had disturbed Time and recalled him back to life, and once even promised to help the Hawklords with their battle. But he remained just as miserable and uncommunicative, and they eventually realized that he was as far from being master of his own fate and actions as ever he had been. He would not move from the Vault, so they left him there. Occasionally they heard the sound of his weeping, and they heard him call the names of his sister, Cymoril, now forever lost, and his one-time trusted companion, Moonglum. "If the Queens can recall me to life, they can take me back!" he moaned out loud, as the Hound Master passed by. His red eyes blazed from between the pure white strands of his hair. "They could have resurrected my friends at least!"

The Hawklord frowned thoughtfully. The manner of the albino had grown so strange that the Hawklords were not at all certain who's side he would eventually choose to fight on.

He walked round one of the stage buttresses with its wrecked searchlight and came to the area that had been reserved as a hospital.

Here, the prone figures of the Children lay.

Ever since he and the Captain had disconnected the automatic broadcasting equipment, in a desperate measure to halt their senseless rampaging, they had lain in a coma brought on by the unguarded exposure to the Death Rays. Their numbers had been reduced to no more than a hundred. They had been laid in rows, and were attended by the white-coated Earth Scientists who walked up and down among them. Occasionally, the Scientists stopped to check a pulse rate, feel a fevered brow or to administer more of the sedative prepared by the Princess who had now reached them with a fresh supply of the saving.

"They all need another dose," Chloral, the Chief Biochemist of the group of Scientists shouted out to her above the roar of the music. He was a plump, bearded man, with bright, twinkling eyes and a quick mind. But he glared at the giant shapes of the vibrating speaker cabinets piled on the stage. "Can't we do anything about the noise?" he asked.

"Sorry," the Princess replied. "You know what'll happen if we turn it down too much."

The Scientist nodded knowingly. "Just trying," he said. He took hold of the jug of solution and began pouring it into glass beakers. He beckoned to the drummer, "If you come here, you'll have to help," he smiled, good-naturedly. He offered Hound Master one of the beakers. "You start at that end."

The Hound Master took hold of the proffered vessel, and did as the scientist instructed. He began raising the heads of the Children and tilting them, forcing the pain killer down their throats.

The Scientists knew about the existence of the Ghost Astronauts, and they had realized straight away that the Children's minds had been invaded. The Ghosts had invaded Elric and when he had arrived in the City they had invaded everyone else in a hopeless attempt to get back their lost bodies. They had been mere pawns in the overall scheme of the Red Queen's and instead of appreciating their new bodies, they had been forced to destroy them — and to destroy everything that the unwilling hosts had made. Swiftly, the Scientists had acted, and exorcised the parasitic life-forms. They had cast them back into the beingless limbo from which they had been evoked — this time for ever.

Unhappily, the Hound Master drained the beaker and looked along the rows of figures. They were coming round.

Soon, they would revive, their minds healed. But they would awake to find an even more unbearable pain.

Grieved, he found himself thinking that they should be allowed to die. But they constituted all that remained of mortal Humanity, and they had to be kept alive. They had to suffer, until every possible avenue of hope had been exhausted.

Kings of Speed erupted from the speakers. A surge of power filled the Hawklord, and he felt the stirrings of the older, restless Hawk spirit inside him. Of all the band members, he was the most sensitive to the psychic fighting powers. Now they tugged at his mind, drawing it back into the dim remote Past where the first battle with the deathly powers of the Generator had taken place. There his soul took refreshment, and he laughed out loud.

LEDGE OF DARKNESS

The wind grew colder around the Hound Master's body and the air grew crisper with increased electrical charge. A giddy, drowsy feeling welled up from inside him. He felt the presence of the Hawk God and let himself relax so that he could pass through the barriers and enter the unknown place where the God resided.

"So!" he shouted out deliriously to the God, as his mind spiralled into darkness. "You've come at last!"

His mind began to surface again, and he opened his eyes.

The shimmering expanse of a grassy plain lay somewhere in front of him. With a shock, he recognized the mystical Plain of As, where, long ago, in the First Magical Age, the first Hawklords had battled.

White, cleanly-picked bones lay on the blood-stained grass, showing signs of a recent battle. Overhead in a dark, overcast sky the carrion shapes of giant birds flapped and cried.

"What have you brought me here for?" he demanded angrily.

At first there was no reply. Then a shrouded figure shimmered into existence in front of him. It hung fragilely against the green grass, unable to gain much solidarity.

"Because you have lessons still to learn, Hawklord!" the figure spoke sternly. 'I cannot come easily. It takes up a great deal of effort and time." It paused, struggling to hold itself. "You have not proved very able. I had assumed that you would have defeated the Death Generator by now. But it seems you have been languishing..."

Hound Master gasped.

"Languishing? We had to rebuild the City! I've been looking for the Life Sword..."

"You've spent a hundred and fifty years in idleness. Like the Hawklords of old, you are close to failing. Soon I shall have to let you return to your natural state...which, by now, is dust, and find other men who will help me better. I cannot get to Earth myself. You must act for me!"

The Hound Master felt confused and indignant.

"What can we do? We can only..."

"You could have located the Death Generator and destroyed it. That is the only way that Earth will be freed of her problems. Instead you have let the machine establish yet another Dark Agent!" The figure waved the Hound Master into silence. "It is no use protesting," it gasped weakly. "I haven't got the time to waste arguing. You will *have to* defeat the Red Queen. She is the worst of the Queens. When she collapses, the others will fall...You must stop her realm spreading...I have brought you here because the Plain of As is the only Earth Time Stream left that has not suffered from her meddling. You must destroy her. Leave the Children to fend for themselves. You must find the Life Sword and destroy the Death Generator..."

"But I..." the Hound Master began. "The band...can't you visit them and tell this to them? They don't believe that there is such a thing as the Life Sword...!"

"Ahhh, they scoff at you, Hound Master! I cannot spare the energy to deal with that trifle...you must..."

The God began pulsing. Its figure disappeared and then reappeared again.

"Go!" it shouted. "But, no! Wait! You cannot go just yet...your adversaries...I tried to stop them, but I feel them coming through..."

The Hound Master stared around in alarm.

'What adversaries?" he cried.

"The warriors from the City of Stones...you have met them before. I cannot hold myself here any longer...They will follow you through. You must go through and fight them...then...you...must...fulfil...the Hawkwind Legend."

The white, streaky figure faded away altogether and the Hawklord was left alone on the timeless plain.

He could see the expanse more clearly.

He could see where before his vision had been obscured and a feeling of dread gripped him.

A thin line of mounted figures were approaching in the distance. There were heavily armed. As they drew closer he made out the grim, taut features of their faces, their raised swords flashing in light that streamed down from behind the clouds.

Raising his two music guns in front of him, he ran forward to meet the horsemen.

The turf vibrated with the pounding of the horses' hooves. But then, the vision began to fade. The features of the warriors vanished and he was unable to obtain a close view of them.

The timeless grassland disappeared once more and the image of the hilltop stage began to shake back into existence.

SWORDSMEN OF HELL

The sounds of the powerful Hawkwind music blasting from the malfunctioning cabinets had ceased, silenced by an invisible hand.

An unearthly quiet had fallen, punctuated only by the moans and cries of the luckless Children. They had awoken and were now suffering again the full force of the Death Radiation.

In front of the drummer stood the Crystal Princess, staring fearfully at him.

"It wasn't me..." he began.

He glanced nervously about him. "We better stay with the Children."

The white-coated Earth Scientists were staggering about among their patients, gasping and choking.

Perplexed shouts came from the stage where the other Hawklords had risen to their feet with drawn guns.

From beyond the brow of the hill behind the rows of stricken Children came the sound of thudding hooves and the clatter of steel swords being drawn from their scabbards.

"Run for the stage!" the Hound Master yelled to the Princess. "The Warriors of Stones...they've broken through!"

Riding up from the ruins of the City, the Hell Riders came. They shimmered with metallic blues and greens. Around them pulsated the white glow of negative energy. They did not seem to be a part of the landscape at all, yet they moved across it, the hooves of their bearers scarcely striking the ground.

Angered by the injustice of the Hawk God's words, and frustrated by his ineffectual encounter with the horsemen on the Plain of As, the Hound Master stayed his ground.

Boldly he withdrew his guns and pointed them at the riders. He watched their features for any sign of vulnerability as they advanced, but there appeared to be no way of getting at them. Glass-like armour encased their skins, its surface active with a thousand colours and shadows. Their skull-shaped faces appeared unkillable, to be already visages of corpses dredged out of the pit.

They would need to call on all their bestowed powers if they were to fight off these attackers, and he found himself praying fervently that the Hawk God, in his wrath, hadn't left them short of any.

The horsemen galloped towards the Children, and he watched their advance with bated breath. Impulsively, he ran forward and fired both his guns. But the white sparks of the Hawkwind music bounced harmlessly off the tall shields that the riders carried to protect themselves.

"DON'T KILL THE CHILDREN!" he screamed out. But there was no need to fear this, for the snorting steeds and their masters did not seem to be interested in the helpless figures lying on the ground. They glided smoothly over them, towards the Hound Master and the stage.

The drummer hesitated.

He turned and ran towards the other Hawklords who had massed themselves defensively in front of the music systems.

They waited tensely, music guns drawn, while the Baron and the Sonic Prince tried vainly to discover what had happened to the music systems.

"I don't get it..." the Baron shouted angrily. "The music guns work OK..."

The horsemen had now formed a shallow semi-circle in front of the Hawklords. They numbered more than two dozen. Their horses pawed at the ground and snorted, and their sleek flanks flashed.

The rider in the centre brought its horse forward. It raised its arm to its face and brought it back down again. A hollow, spitting voice issued from behind its helmet. The sound seemed to come from inside the Hawklords' heads, and cut savagely through their minds.

"Do not underestimate us, Hawklings!" the voice scoffed. "Five thousand years ago, and again forty centuries later, you thought you had conquered us! Five *hundred* thousand centuries is not long enough to put between us — and our war will long be over before that time comes! There will be no more war after today! Earth is ours, by right! Prepare to die, Hawklings, for you have lived long enough! Remember...you cannot kill *dead* men!"

The voice laughed emptily as the rider fell back into place.

Then, in unison, all of the horsemen drew forth the mighty, double-bladed swords. In their left hands appeared the tall, golden shields, stamped with the images of snakes and lizards.

Each Hawklord recognized the designs. They had seen them in the Hawkwind book of psalms, *Doremi Fasol Latido*, the ancient manuscript which contained the Hawkwind Legend and which they had once interpreted in a series of chants on their album of the same name. The phantom assailants were the warriors of evil that the giant Lord Atmar had fought vainly to outwit so long ago, and they were also the warriors who had fought earlier manifestations of the Hawklords. Momentarily, the Hawklords wished that they were back at the Phantom Inn where they themselves had first begun changing into the new Hawklords, perusing the pages of the ancient book rather than facing its characters.

The Dark Warrior's words, spoken a moment ago rang in their ears. "Earth is ours, by right!" it had said.

Pictures of the Children, battling for life against starvation, disease and the Death Radiation flashed through their minds. The Image of Earth as they had known her burned inside them all. The feelings of grandeur and power they had felt as the Hawklord warriors of old, coursed through their veins. They knew then, that the ghosts before them *were* vulnerable...like the pinball machine. They were a threat only so long as they believed them to be a threat.

"No! You're wrong!" Captain Calvert screamed out at them. He jumped forward defiantly. "Earth belongs to no one!" He raised his music gun and fired it at the nearest Hell Rider.

A white spark zig-zagged from his arm and struck the creature's shield. It was accompanied by a sharp crack of electricity as the Hawkwind music rent the charged air. The spark struck the shield a ferocious blow. The metal glowed white hot, but withstood the onslaught. The spark was deflected, and the rider stayed firm.

Astounded, the Captain fired his gun again. This time, he aimed it at the rider's head. The rider drew up his shield, with the same result.

Clenching his jaw muscles, the Captain held the gun at arm's length with both hands, and fired a prolonged burst, keeping it trained on the shield. Still the shield withstood the blast.

Dimly, he heard other guns crackling and spitting from beside him, but the resistant shields held firm. With a sinking heart he realized that in some way their musical power had been anticipated.

The line of horsemen came together.

It formed a solid, golden wall.

Slowly, the wall began bearing down on them, moving in the path of the Hawkwind music.

SEA OF ANONIMITY

The gleaming swords of the Riders were now raised high against the sky. Already they were dipped with crimson, though they had not yet taken blood.

"Do your worst!" Thunder Rider mocked them above the roar of the crackling Hawkwind guns. "You'll not kill Hawklords — this time or any other time!"

The Baron and the Sonic Prince gave up the music system as a dead loss and added their power to their beleaguered comrades. From the hill's edge, overlooking the choked deserts and the darkening Time Walls, the Orgasm Band ran to lend their assistance. They had been gigging quietly to themselves in celebration of the dead Steel Eye Skelter. But the Starstreakers, and their powerful music weaponry which could have helped the Hawklords most, lay out of reach, cut off by the advancing horsemen.

The two rock bands turned up their guns to full volume, determined to fight to the bitter end. They hoped that the immense front of energy they released would take its toll. The air filled with the sharp tang of ozone and sulphur. The riders still held firm, but then, whether from impatience or pain, one of the horsemen broke the line.

Captain Calvert saw his chance to penetrate behind the golden barrier of shields and courageously threw himself to the ground beside the oncoming steed. The white, brimmed hat he had been wearing rolled beneath the tirade of hooves. He aimed his music gun at the exposed rider's flank and fired.

The gun played *You'd Better Believe It*.

The fiery bolt struck home before the creature inside the armour could protect itself. It shrieked hollowly and its ghostly body dissipated into the air. The empty shell of its armour toppled from its saddle and crashed to the earth.

Twisting round, he played a second shot from the same track at one of the two horsemen he now found himself lying between. Their shield had swept round to face him, and the fierce blast of Hawkwind music was unwittingly deflected and amplified between them. With an unearthly cry, they too fell, in pain and rage, and flashed out of existence. Their panicking steeds stampeded toward the group of Hawklords, but their outlines faded away before they reached them.

Surprised, the Hawklords took up the swords of the departed ghosts. They began hacking and chopping at the mounted figures. The warriors from before Time fought back, and now the feuders were evenly matched. The air filled with the sound of clanging, tortured metal.

The Captain raised himself to his feet and ran through the gap he had made in the horsemen's line. He came up from behind them, and began spraying the area ahead of him with sound.

The gun had changed tracks and was now playing *Seeing It As You Really Are*.

In confusion, the weakened riders turned round to face their new threat. As they did so they were caught in the back by the Hawklords' guns firing from the stage.

They became disorderly. Their lurid hues grew dimmer, and their outlines blazed with an unhealthy intensity as the lethal doses of energy they were forced to absorb saturated their systems and burned off them.

The scene became a blazing pin-point of white light. It pulsated strongly for a moment, and then faded away to nothing.

Where the Horsemen had once stood, only the faintest smell of brimstone remained.

The Hawklords stood frozen, their guns still sparking through the air. Abruptly, the speakers on stage crackled back to life as mysteriously as they had cut out. The Hawklords turned their hand weapons off.

"The Children!" The Crystal Princess was the first of them to react. She began to run forward in alarm, but Captain Calvert restrained her.

"Leave the Children to Patti and the Scientists..." he cried, his eyes alight. He looked from face to face among the stunned assembly. "The Hawk God is right! We must leave them to fend for themselves!"

He turned his head away abruptly, and his finely-profiled face stared painfully at the towering Time Zones.

They followed his gaze.

While the music supply from the stage had been cut off, the grey walls had moved closer to the hill. The daylight had grown more gloomy still, and the meaningless changing flotsam of humanity had submerged the blackened ruins. Now the Sea of Anonimity lapped at the very edge of their dwindling realm, threatening to engulf and render them also meaningless.

"We must stop trying to rebuild the City..." Captain Calvert continued. "It's hopeless doing that until the Death Generator has been defeated! We must attack the Queens as we planned, and then, Hound Master," he turned to the drummer, "we must find the Life Sword."

The Hawklords stood uncomfortably, their minds awash with the implications of his words. In their hearts they knew that no other course of action was open to them. If they didn't act immediately, Earth City and life as they knew it would perish. The impatient forces that moved and moaned around them would claim their long-awaited victory.

HEARTBREAK SEA

The small fleet of craft and the winged Beast buffeted and shook in the winds caused by the growing Time Zones as they rose once more from the crumbling hilltop.

The Zones bulged and glowed ominously, sucking in heat from the surrounding air as the Hawklords veered away into the thunderous sky. They were waved off by the Boss, the Dealer, Patti and the white-coated Earth Scientists…the rear-guard of attacking Humanity who would follow when their ranks had recovered.

The day turned chill beneath the full sun, and below them as they flew, the mixed-up world of men and monsters seethed and cried in anguish.

Impassively, the Hawklords flew on above the heartbreak sea.

They left behind the tiny island of sanity and hope they had come from, trusting that it would hold off the Enemy Force for a short while longer.

They approached the dwarfing mass of the parent Time Zone of Deliria.

It hung before them, vast and formidable. Although still some miles away, it seemed to lie only a few inches from them. Its veined, marble-like expanse filled their vision as they streaked silently towards it, their size dwindling away to nothing.

It began shining brilliantly, blinding them with its light again.

The air round about them grew freezing cold as the Zone expanded outwards, growing even vaster.

This time the Hawklords were not deterred. They continued to advance until at last the mists claimed them, and they gazed once again through the twilight air of Deliria.

KERB CRAWLER

They arrived somewhere in the heart of the great West Coast City, at a massive intersection.

In front of them ran a crumbling, six-lane main street. At one time built to cater for the needs of millions of San Franciscan motorists, it was now virtually deserted. Along its central island ran the tracks of the electric trams, of which there was now no sign. Its sidewalks were thinly populated with mutants dressed in shabby overcoats, who shuffled along, keeping close to the store fronts and the sides of the buildings for protection.

'Market Street," Astral Al informed the Hawklords in silent awe. "The Zone's grown. We've entered Frisco on the opposite side to Playland…this is Downtown…"

He looked towards a large road that crossed the bottom of the street at right angles. "That's the Embarcadero…it runs along the Bay and the docks," he told them. "That's the start of the Bay Bridge." He pointed out a looming, reinforced concrete structure that cut across the featureless sky. "That goes out to Oakland…" He looked up at the tall building with a clock tower that sat at the foot of the intersection — under better conditions a graceful building, spoilt only by an ugly motorway flyover which had thoughtlessly been built in front of it. "The Ferry Building," the Hawklord continued. "It's just as well I know this bit of the city for reference reasons. When we need to get out we just fly in the direction of that clock tower…"

"Where's the Red Queen?" the Baron asked. He and the other Hawklords who were new to Deliria looked at the recreated city with mixed feelings. It reminded them sharply of their own past, and they were filled with conflicting emotions — nostalgia, grief, fear and bewilderment.

Leprus, the giant winged Beast, crouched low on the ground, its eyes glinting with a silvery light. It seemed paralyzed by excitement, affected by the thinly ionized air.

"Easy, boy" its Master spoke to it distractedly, scratching its chin whilst he gazed around him. "It's all right boy."

Captain Calvert adjusted his cravat to gain more air in the claustrophobic stillness. Rashly or not, they all now wore their casual clothes again. The desert suits had proved uncomfortable on the long missions. It had been too much of an effort to resist the unspoken decision to discard them, for their minds had lost interest in all but the one consuming goal of destruction.

"We don't know how the Red Queen will choose to receive us this time," Lord Rudolph informed the Baron. "Last time she made us welcome in a most beguiling manner."

"So we heard," the Crystal Princess spoke huffily. "She won't try the same tricks twice, you know. I can tell you that...speaking from another woman's point of view."

"We'd better proceed with what we intended," Thunder Rider advised. "We can't wait for her to decide what she's going to do about us."

"Then we head towards Playland," Astral Al decided. "With any luck the fairgroundsman we saved will still have a juice supply. If we can set up at his place we'll be close to where Patti said the Transmogrifier is located."

He patted his pocket where the Light Lord's music tape was safely stored. "Then we'll be ready to feed in this."

"Let's hope she was right," the Light Lord said. He gripped the bar of his Starstreaker in readiness. "How do we get there from here?"

"Don't worry about that," Astral Al grinned. "I think I still know the way — by cab at least, so I should be able to find it by air."

Cautiously, they began to rise on their Starstreakers, thankful to leave the presence of the mutants and be out of sight of the occasional darkened cars that swished by.

VORTEX OF DEATH

"Still no sign of the cops," Thunder Rider reported. His voice carried clearly through the heavy, motionless atmosphere as they passed over the big city. The tops of tall skyscrapers rose up to meet them, standing like silent steel and glass sentinels up and down the steep Frisco hills. The buildings were unlit and unused. Like the pyramids, they seemed to be on the verge of crumbling, yet oddly they remained intact.

Ahead lay the large hill separating the city's Bay area from its Haight-Ashbury suburb. They headed towards the peak, keeping as close together as they could, watchfully scanning the sinister scene below them.

"You spoke too soon, I think," the Light Lord commented. "I can feel that music coming from somewhere."

He shivered and sunk his head in his shoulders. He had been aware of the unpleasant sensations for some time, but they had only just registered on his conscious mind. The other Hawklords felt them.

"Uh! Where are they coming from?" Captain Calvert asked. A look of distaste appeared on his face. "Do they get any worse?"

"Plenty," Lord Rudolph told him. He looked down again at the ground. "Look! The place is full of Bulls!"

They looked down from their silver flying machines through the light of the Hawk aura that shone from their bodies. They were passing over a large hospital block and a small park on the mountain's crest. On the hospital's roof, and swarming through the surrounding trees and bushes were the figures of the motorcycle squad. Their helmeted and sunglassed faces were looking upward and they held what looked like shields and riot sticks. Rising faintly on the air the Hawklords could hear the jarring sound of their tape recorders.

From other parts of the city came the roar of engines and the wailing police sirens.

A convoy of lorries, enormous Mack trucks, appeared, winding its way at top speed up Roosevelt Way from the Noe Valley. It was flanked by columns of Bulls mounted on their growling Harleys. Each lorry was equipped with a huge, swivel loudspeaker cone, mounted like an evil eye on its cabin roof, and pulled behind it an amplifier on a trailer the size of a small house.

Thunder Rider whistled. "You were right, Princess. She never plays the same tricks twice. If they play those things before we get our band set up, we've had it!"

The Dark Music began to erode their senses, and they lost height. It sapped away their strength, sucking them down like a magnet.

"Cannons, fire!" Captain Calvert commanded.

Without having to be asked twice, the Hawk pilots did as they were bid. Their craft became enveloped in crackling globules of light, and they were able to pull away from the city, and cross the hill.

Soon, they were streaking across the rooftops of Haight-Ashbury, hell bent to reach the fairgroundsman in time.

They passed again over the fiery pit of the Kezar Stadium. It glowed sullenly beneath them, stoked by the Ghouls whose meaningless tasks released their vital life energies to the parasitic Queens.

They flew above the rooftops of the Science Museum and the Japanese Tea Gardens in Golden Gate Park, and skimmed low over the compounds and cages where the mutant slaves were kept.

At last they came to the wreckage of the derelict pleasure complex.

Unlike their last visit to Playland, they did not care much about being seen. This time they flew loftily and proudly. They quickly noticed the lone light of the fairgroundsman's Waltzer radiating boldly from among the ruins.

Gratefully, they glided towards it.

But their assailants had not been slow either. They had sped freely along the deserted highways, and from the direction of the gates leading to the pleasure land came the sudden roar of their bikes.

The disquieting notes of the Dark Music sounded again. The high-powered music blared out at them, eroding away their minds.

Valiantly, the nine, brightly-burning stars of light curved in a gentle arc towards the Waltzer. They landed in time to dismount and unload some of the equipment, their music cannons still blaring at full intensity. But the Hawkwind music was of insufficient power to match the combined broadcasts coming from the hordes of Ghouls.

"It's no good, we'll never get it all assembled in time!" the Light Lord shouted. Desperately, he struggled with the black cube of a Delatron, an object that was normally weightless in his mighty Hawk grasp. He let it fall clumsily to the wooden walkway that surrounded the Waltzer.

Dizzily, he sat down and with ailing senses tried to make out what was happening round about him.

The Waltzer's lights were full on, emitting silver rays into the unhealthy, bluish plasma. Its ridged deck with the bucket seats was motionless. Its gaudy colouring appeared monochrome in the shadowless conditions. There was no sign of the fairgroundsman, who had possibly seen the Hawklords coming and retreated into the ruins for safety.

The Light Lord's thoughts seemed to come to him with difficulty, across a great gulf of space.

Despairing, he realized that their mission had been badly planned due to the haste with which they had been forced to act.

Dimly, he made out the shapes of the other Hawklords labouring under the strain of their work. Then he noticed the first of the mounted police appearing around the corner of the access track.

When the Bulls saw the Hawklords they brought their machines to a screeching halt. They dismounted, settled their bikes on their kickstands, and advanced forward. Their tape recorders were drawn and playing, sending out jagged fingers of energy.

More Bulls burst into view, and they too dismounted and advanced.

Spreading out, circling the Waltzer, they cut the Hawklords off and surrounded them with a field of force.

The last refuge of the Hawklords became a sphere of burning light almost impossible to see through.

Through its fierceness their dying gaze made out the giant form of Colonel Goodnight.

He stood closer to the Hawkwind music than his misshapen companions, able to withstand the onslaught of the Hawkwind waves far more readily than they.

He was clad in gleaming armour. His helmeted, cylindrical head rotated from side to side, eyes blazing fiercely out at them through slits in the metal. On his shoulder he carried a massive, bazooka-like music gun which he pointed at them. He moved it slowly and intently from side to side, spraying their shrinking sphere with lethal tunes — *Daniel*, by Elton John; *Lady Samantha*, by Elton John; *Your Song*, by Elton John; *Take Me to The Pilot*, by Elton John; *Border Song*, by Elton John; *Honky Cat*, by Elton John...

On and on came the tunes, changing rapidly, a medley of forbidden vapid songs and trite melodies battering at their senses.

The Hawk power broke under the combined assault. The ring the Ghouls had made gradually closed in.

But a dying thought had formed in the Light Lord's mind, and he rose from where he had fallen.

He looked drunkenly around him, then climbed unsteadily on the Waltzer, oblivious of the now prostrate Hawklords behind him and the unattended music cannons still blazing away. He knew only that he had to do what he did. If time ran out then at least he had tried.

He wandered stiffly across the Waltzer's undulated platform.

Momentarily, he blacked out and fell.

He came to again. With single-minded perseverance he climbed to his feet. He discovered that he had fallen inside the control cockpit where the fairgroundsman lived.

The flicker of a smile crossed his taut features.

The mutant was not there, but that didn't matter.

He leant against the shelf supporting the control board and looked around with glazed eyes. Somewhere nearby there ought to be an amplifier.

He put his hands out and felt along the shelf. Immediately beneath them lay the twin turntables of the Waltzer's powerful loudspeaker disco assembly.

Fumbling along the output wire with his fingers, he traced it round the bench to a shelf behind him. Hazily, he looked down at the large solid frontage of the amplifier.

It was a coarser instrument than any that Hawkwind had ever used. But it would do.

His energy picked up slightly, and he bent down and pulled it, fraction by fraction out of its housing. He lifted the butt off his still functioning music gun and extracted the carefully folded extension lead from inside. The output end of the wire was affixed to the tiny Delatron inside; the other end was fitted with a standard DIN plug.

Sluggishly, he jerked away the output wire from the record decks and inserted the lead from his music gun in its place.

Through a haze of pain, he forced one arm in front of the other and managed to push the heavy instrument back into its place.

He pressed the "On" switch.

He prayed that juice was available. But no sound came out.

Fighting for his life, he staggered out of the control box, intending to locate the main switch he knew must be near at hand. A deadening blackness suddenly engulfed his wracked body.

He slumped forward, prey to the numbing Music of Darkness that tore at his mind for the last time.

JOURNEY BEYOND THE EDGE OF TIME

Angrily, the dealer slammed the card down on the card table. The table shook and creaked.

"The Red Queen!" he shouted, a look of utter despair on his face. "Look at it! My boys, my boys..." he wept. "They've had it. She's won! I knew she'd win..." He went off into a long tirade of accusations and oaths.

"Shut up!" the Boss yelled at him. "You're making everyone nervous."

Scientists, Children. Orgasm Band, Boss and Dealer now sat on the stage at Parliament Hill. They were surrounded by the enveloping walls of the Time Zones which expanded perilously close to the hill's edge. The suffocating debris of past existence pushed itself up from the plain below and spilled on their island. The Children had revived, due to the improved sounds coming from the repaired equipment, but they were still in a bad way, and in fear of the journey they now had to undergo.

"The hill is no longer safe," Patti declared. "We had better get going while we can."

"No one moves until I say so," the Boss told her, standing his ground firmly. "We had a time limit and I'm gonna see everyone sticks to it."

He stared at Patti. She looked as beautiful as ever, and he yearned to declare his secret love for her but he knew that this was not the right time. He swallowed. "If we go too soon we might balls up their operation," he explained in a gentler voice.

Everyone stayed where they were.

They waited, although there seemed nothing left worth waiting for.

Eventually, the Boss raised his arm in the air and scrutinized his watch. It didn't register the "correct" time, for there was no chronological time kept in Earth City, but it was at least an indicator of elapsed minutes in times of emergency.

He climbed to his feet. "It's time," he said.

As one, the population rose to their feet.

The Boss and the Dealer took the lead and they began to file slowly down the approach road into the shifting debris below. They clutched music guns and the few musical instruments they had managed to lay their hands on. At the rear, the Orgasm Band flew on their Starstreakers, playing their music cannons. When the small army of Children left the shelter of the stage they would at least have some respite from the battering they would receive from the Death Generator's Rays.

Hopefully, some would survive to help in the final battle inside Deliria.

The Dealer looked back hesitantly at the stage.

"Elric..." he began. "We can't leave him..."

"He's had his chances," the Boss replied without turning. "He could have come if he wanted."

They continued onward, marching downhill.

From behind they could still hear the stage music. No one really expected to see this last outpost of Earth City again, but they had left the Hawkwind music playing as a temporary symbol of their existences amid the engulfing Death World.

Now, they had reached the jungle of human flotsam confusedly flashing in and out of existence in front of them. They plunged into it, putting their lives at risk.

The Dealer laughed, deriving a peculiar happiness from the circumstances. Still laughing, he reached for his cigar.

But it wasn't there.

And from far behind came a long, loud moan.

It wailed through the roaring sounds of Chaos.

Inside the Time Vault the albino had awoken from his gloom. He sprang to his feet, eyes flashing now with a new fire. In his hand, Stormbringer writhed with pleasure and the promise of souls.

It moaned, long and loud.

RELEASE FROM BONDAGE

The Presence shivered with ecstasy.

It warmed and glowed all over as the life energies of despair and suffering throughout the Universe came to it and were absorbed.

She laughed, and the ripples spread out along her body which now seemed to occupy the Universe.

Soon, she would *be* the Universe.

The Time Streams began to collapse.

She would be all that *was*.

There would be no Time.

She would be God.

Soon...

Her mind flashed to long ago, when she had started out on her hard and lonely rise to power.

She had not known then what she knew now, though in the small child's mind there had always lain the vague, unresolved ambition that had made her fight so hard.

The tall, handsome figure of a man walked with her on the way to a candy store on a street corner in New Jersey.

The man smiled at her and bent down to pick her up and show her the candies in the window.

"You like that one?" his muted voice asked her.

"Oh, Dad!" she cried in longing, now in the present. "Oh, Dad, Dad, Dad! I want *that* one! I *want* that one!"

She clasped her fat hands to her swirling being that had expanded and grown to fill everywhere and have everything.

But the dark hint of a threat came to spoil her triumphant pleasure.

Back there, long ago, had been the figure of *another*. A *woman*.

A car drew up outside the candy store and a graceful, not pretty woman climbed out, breathing perfume, and stood next to them and put her arms around her father. She told him to put the child down.

The Red Queen's memories were snuffed out.

Angrily, she screamed at the lingering face of the woman.

"Mommy, you bitch! Mother, you…"

But she stopped herself and smiled.

She wallowed in Space.

Her being drifted sweetly through Time.

The barriers were collapsing. There were no more things she could not have, and now she *had* what her mother had.

She laughed again and again. Her happiness overflowed to maim and destroy and kill all it touched.

The feeling of destiny hadn't deserted her.

It still lay inside and now she was at a loss to understand why it hadn't been satisfied. It had driven her so far, and she had risen to conquer all.

Yet she still wanted.

The thought shattered the brief respite she had won from the loneliness of struggling…

ROCKING CAROUSEL

Veils of darkness seemed to hang in front of the Light Lord's eyes.

His body felt like raw meat. He screamed up from the well of dark that enveloped him.

Gradually, his vision cleared.

The world was spinning round crazily. Violent emotions threw his limp body from side to side against hard metal bars and walls of iron. A thudding noise battered at his ears. Long wailing notes and sliding guitar sounds tore away parts of his mind.

The Waltzer was in full motion.

Somehow he had managed to fall inside one of the spinning seats. Groggily, he remembered what had happened, and he realized thankfully that it was his music gun that was playing over the roundabout's powerful speakers.

It was playing *Magnu*, a Brock composition.

But who had turned the juice on?

He tried to prop himself up in the gyrating, bouncing chair, but was thrown breathlessly back in his seat again by something soft falling heavily across him.

Confused, he pushed at the soft weight.

It slid away back to the opposite end of the seat. It was the corpse of one of the Ghouls who must have tried to stop him operating the Waltzer.

It had been killed outright by the sudden increase in the volume of the Hawkwind music. It lolled lifelessly, backwards and forwards.

Throwing back the chrome safety bar of the bucket seat, he hauled himself unsteadily to his feet.

He jumped out on to the revolving platform. It swept him up and down, and he stumbled and rolled dangerously close to another of the whirling seats. He managed to climb upright once more, and jumped back into the control cockpit. He found a lever marked "Emergency Stop" which he guessed operated the motors. He pulled it down and with a shriek, audible above the noise of the music, the Waltzer began to slow down.

The Light Lord heaved a sigh of relief. Now, he was able to concentrate on what had happened outside.

He ran out the door and off the Waltzer.

Colonel Goodnight and his Ghouls had pulled back, leaving their bikes and many of their bodies strewn about in front of the hills of masonry and scrap metal.

The other Hawklords were lying on the ground, their Starstreakers lying at their sides, their equipment scattered about at random. The ragged, faithful Leprus looked distinctly worried. It pecked forlornly at its Master and glared suspiciously at another figure that was kneeling nearby.

The Light Lord recognized the fairgroundsman, and his first impulse was to pull out his music gun and shoot him.

Then he remembered that his music gun was playing over the Waltzer. Besides which, the mutant seemed to be helping them.

"They OK?" he shouted instead.

He drew closer, puzzled by the mutant's ability to exist so close to the Hawkwind music.

The creature turned. Its face was covered with the unpleasant bubbly-skin affliction, but the Light Lord was able to sense from its eyes that its mind was far from mutated. He was facing an ally.

"They're coming round," the fairgroundsman replied. "You want to see?" He stood aside.

The Light Lord frowned and walked over. He knelt down by the side of his friends. He noticed that their bodies had been positioned neatly. Their jackets had been rolled up and placed thoughtfully beneath their heads.

He put his ear to each of their hearts, and then arose, relieved.

'Thanks," he said to the mutant. "Was it you who turned on the amplifier?"

The mutant nodded. "I watched you come in, and I saw what you were trying to do with your...that device you have. Only thing is, I turned the whole lot on. I'd forgot you were still in the seat..."

"You're not affected by our music," the Light Lord stated. "You look..." He trailed off.

The other shuffled uncomfortably and looked down at this feet. He wore a pair of ragged jeans, frayed at the ankles, and a roughened brown leather jacket with the collar turned up. On his head he wore a large straw hat and on his feet, tall, painted boots.

He spoke bitterly. "That whore...until all this happened..." He waved his arms aggressively in the air. ". . . I looked like you. Normal and human. But don't be fooled by that. She hasn't managed to screw up my head like the rest of them."

The Light Lord felt sorry for the man. "Who are you?" he asked.

"Nothing, nothing," the man replied. "Just a hired hand. I was a nobody. Still am, I guess. But I've not given in like they have. I couldn't do that."

"You've got guts," the Light Lord told him.

A groan came from the floor. They looked down. Thunder Rider was trying to sit up. They stooped and helped him to his feet. He gazed uncomprehendingly at them until his memory returned and he managed to smile.

"So we made it..." he said, a faint smile on his lips. He leaned heavily on the Light Lord. "You're the fairgroundsman, aren't you?" he asked the mutant.

The man nodded, smiling tightly. "What we used to call a roustabout."

Briefly the Light Lord explained what had happened. As he spoke, the other Hawklords began to recover and they too rose to their feet. After they had learnt what had happened they thanked the Light Lord for his presence of mind, and paid their respects to their new friend.

"You're welcome," the fairgroundsman replied. "But I owed you the favour from last time. I'd have been sunk if it wasn't for you."

"The amazing thing is you aren't dead already," Thunder Rider told him, bending down to try and clear his head. By degrees, the Hawk strength returned to him.

"I would have been, but they've been leaving me alone..." He paused thoughtfully. "Must be because you're here. Say, who are you?"

"Too little time to explain, but you'll get to know," the Hawklord told him. "Let's just say we're on your side." He turned to the others who were now looking much better. "We better get the equipment together," he said gravely. "When those large lorries carrying the speakers arrive, they'll be able to neutralize this lot with ease." Another thought occurred to him and he turned worriedly to face the fairgroundsman. "All they've got to do to defeat us is cut off the juice supply."

"Not now, they can't!" The man grinned. "I used to steal what I needed from their main cable supplies, but they got wise! They detected me. Since you helped me out that time, I've been using a generator. Now I'm stealing their gasoline!" he laughed.

"How much petrol have we got?" the Light Lord asked.

The fairgroundsman's face grew serious. "Not that much, I'm afraid. I was gonna get some more when you arrived. We've got enough to last a coupla hours."

"A couple of hours!" the Crystal Princess blurted out in alarm. "How far away is the Presidio?" she asked Astral Al.

The drummer shrugged. "Not too far..."

"It's about an hour on foot," the fairgroundsman told them. He looked incredulously at them. "You planning on going *there?*"

"That's where the Transmogrifier is located," the Baron told him short-temperedly, "according to this lot." He looked around at them all disdainfully. "We've ballsed-up," he said. "It's going to take an hour to set up the equipment. By the time one of us reaches the Transmogrifier with the tape it'll be too late to do anything."

"The Presidio though..." the mutant continued, not wishing to involve himself in their argument. ". . . That's where the Queens hang out. You'll never get in..."

"If we can get our music going properly you'll be surprised what we can get into!" Astral Al told him. He started. "Where they *live*, you say? But..."

"That's what I said," the fairgroundsman interrupted him. "That's where the Queens are based…for the time being anyhow. They plan to move to Washington as soon as it's ready."

The drummer turned back to the Hawklords. "Patti never told us that." He grinned. "That makes our job easier."

"You're joking!" Captain Calvert exclaimed. "It makes it more difficult. If they're in there…they'll defend it…"

"It makes them more easy to *kill*," Astral Al smiled ironically. "When we know where they are."

This time the fairgroundsman looked at the Hawklords with disbelief. "*Kill* them?" he asked. "You're here to *kill* them?" He laughed manically. "Now I know you've got to be…unreal…" He put his hands to his head. "I never thought you were real in the first place." He sat down on the edge of the Waltzer, and shook his head.

But the Hawklords did not hear him. They began collecting their scattered instruments from the floor as they argued. They unloaded the Delatrons and amplifiers from their Starstreakers.

Lord Rudolph shouted out angrily. "My Gibson…it's been scratched!" He held up the black *Boneshiverer* and ran his fingers over the marks.

"So long as it plays…" the Light Lord shouted back.

Lord Rudolph glared at him indignantly. "It's all very well for you to talk like that. All your equipment's been smashed!"

They worked on tensely, slowly connecting their equipment.

The Baron led the disbelieving fairgroundsman away to find the generator, and together they hefted it to the make-shift stage.

Captain Calvert helped the Hound Master assemble his drums, while the Sonic Prince attended to the Delatrons. He also tried to fathom a way of integrating the Waltzer's amplification system with their own.

It took them as long as the Baron had said it would to set up, but at length they were ready.

As they were about to take up their positions, the flickering light emanating from the hordes of Enemy tape-recorders in the junk hills seemed to increase wildly.

Alarmed, the Hawklords peered into the perpetual twilight of the Death World.

THE RUSHING SPIRES

Along the congested track leading into the Playland complex moved three intensely bright spindles of light.

The spindles radiated abnormal amounts of light energy and spun coldly on their axes, enveloping darker, upright figures that moved inside them. The figures and their rotating cocoons glided several feet above the ground, avoiding the fallen motorbikes and the police corpses that lay in their path.

"The Queens!" the fairgroundsman shrieked in terror. "They're coming through!"

Astral Al laid an arm on his shoulder. "Keep cool. They can't do much, otherwise they wouldn't have those fields around them."

"What do they want?" Thunder Rider asked. "Get ready to repel them in case they try anything."

While the spindles of light glided closer to them, they picked up their instruments. The spindles got within a few yards of the group and then stopped. The force fields dimmed slightly, then stabilized themselves.

"Hawklords!" the leading figure spoke to them above the roar of the Hawkwind music. Its voice was not loud yet it communicated clearly to them and they had no difficulty in recognizing the feminine tones. "I've come to strike a bargain with you!"

Beneath their white mantles of light, the figures of the Queens shimmered and curled hatefully, their colours indiscernible in the monochrome landscape.

"There's no bargain we can strike with you!" Captain Calvert yelled out. "We've come here to destroy you and we mean to do it!"

"Hawklords, listen to me. You cannot escape this time. We are gathering to defeat you, and soon we will have the power we need. Even if you survive this, it is only a question of time before you fuel runs out and your music stops. Then you will die!"

The leading spindle grew a silvery psuedopodium and indicated the figure on its left.

"This is the Black Queen of Clubs...She is the Queen of Alaska. The Transmogrifier finished recreating Alaska yesterday," the Red Queen's voice told them. The spindle that was the Queen of Clubs glowed extra brightly with pleasure. "And here is my rival, the Queen of Hearts." The Red Queen indicated the spindle on her right. The spindle shone warmly. "She is the Queen of Alabama...a later development. Alabama was recreated only this morning! So you see, the Transmogrifier is doing its job. Three entire States now exist and several more are on the way. They're not yet linked together, but I expect the joining up to take place tomorrow…" She paused, and added seriously, "As a result of this, your Time Stream has unfortunately been disrupted. If you were to return now, you would not survive long."

"How kind of you to let us know," Lord Rudolph told her with distaste. "But your Highness really does underestimate our power. It is we who have the upper hand this time. You *know* that and you're just trying to trick us into giving in. But seeing as you've given us the honour of your visit, you might as well let us know your proposition."

The spindle pulsed madly for a few moments, then subsided again. The Queen's voice had none of the crooning qualities that had marked it on earlier occasions. "I have come, Hawklords, to offer you an alternative to death."

"And what could you possibly offer us?" Astral Al asked her scornfully.

"Join me!" the voice beseeched them. "We can consolidate our power and share the task of ruling the planet equally…"

The Hawklords stared at her in puzzlement.

"Join *you?*" the Crystal Princess cried out. She fumed at the idea. "We wouldn't join you, you disgusting old crone! Our people have suffered for thousands of years from the Death Generator. Most of them have died for their beliefs at the hands of such as you! And now you ask us to join you? Get stuffed!" she retorted angrily. "We'd rather die fighting you now than join you and perish later…for that's what will happen to you in the end. Your policies of death and destruction will lead to death and destruction for you and Deliria. They will eventually destroy everything by their very nature. Life cannot exist without a balance and you offer it none. When you have conquered and governed everything, what then, Red Queen?"

There was an unexpected silence.

A heavy sadness radiated off the leading spindle and the Hawklords looked at each other, confused.

The spindle moved forward slightly. The two Heads of State at its side dimmed, allowing it to outshine them.

As the Hawklords watched, the force field surrounding the Red Monarch disappeared abruptly. In its place stood the young beautiful woman they had seen with the President in the newsreel clips.

There were tears on her cheeks.

Her luxuriant hair was tousled and her clothes looked creased and crumpled.

Thunder Rider swallowed. She looked no older than Patti and he tried to fight down the paternal instincts her presence aroused in him.

The young woman trembled and looked at the Princess.

"You are right," she said sadly. "There is nothing left for me…I've been wrong all along. I've…killed your people…" She began crying openly. "I've been arrogant. I've been the death of decent life, and now the Earth itself. I didn't mean to do it! I'm sorry...I'm sorry!" She sobbed uncontrollably. She got a grip on her emotions again. "What can I do now? Your music is more powerful than mine. I tried to stop you, but you got through. I knew when you escaped from me last time that if you returned it would be all over. I hope you will be lenient with me. I beg you not to hurt me...I...I'll try to put things right again," she stammered.

The Hawklords listened, gripped by the emotional outburst.

"She's saying the exact opposite of what she was saying a moment ago!" Thunder Rider exclaimed in surprise. "But you *can't* put things right now," he told her forcibly. "You've already gone too far." He turned to the others. "What do we do? We can't kill her if she's asking for mercy."

"It's a cheap trick!" the Crystal Princess retorted. "If you believe her, Thunder Rider, you'll believe anything. She's frightened of us. She's failed to frighten us and now she's trying another ploy. Don't listen to her. Start the live music now."

The tearful woman shied away. "NO!" she cried in evident horror. "Can't you see I'm already withstanding your music...I've dropped my shield, to try and show you that I'm being sincere."

"If you really want to make up for what you've done, stop the Transmogrifier," Astral Al told her mercilessly.

The woman hung her head,

"I can't" she said.

"What?" the Baron cried out. "You must be able to!"

"No," she replied. "It's out of my control. It's working on its own."

"She's lying!" the Light Lord shouted. "Thunder Rider, the Princess is right. We must start playing. While the Red Queen's stalling us, those Ghouls of hers are building up reinforcements. You saw those lorries..."

Except for the saxophonist, they began to position themselves, ready to play. The Sonic Prince unplugged the Light Lord's music gun from the Waltzer's amplifier and replaced it with the lead from his electric violin.

There was a deep and deadening silence as the taped Hawkwind music ceased. They felt the crippling force of the Dark Music strike at their minds.

Then the Hound Master began drumming.

He drummed wildly and powerfully, just as though he had not been away from his drum kit.

And the beautiful young lady began screaming.

She screamed in agony, clutching at her hair and face as giant sparks leapt out from the band towards her.

She began crumpling to the floor, unable to withstand the onslaught of sound and fire. The two spindles of light at her side glowed fiercely behind their protective shields and deserted her, unable to face the battering.

"NO!" she screamed. "NO! YOU'RE KILLING ME!"

Tight-lipped, the Sonic Prince brought his violin up under his chin and began playing. Next, Lord Rudolph came in on *Boneshiverer*, and then the Baron on *Godblaster*. Captain Calvert brought the microphone he was holding up to his lips. In front of the drum kit the Crystal Princess began dancing frenetically.

Soon, the full thunderous sound of *Assault and Battery* was being driven out, shaking the ground and rattling the heaps of the broken funfair machinery with its intensity.

Thunder Rider looked on, horrified at the apparent callousness of his friends.

But, abruptly the writhing, tortured figure of the Red Queen began to change its shape.

As he watched, it grew older.

Its smooth, voluptuous face became wrinkled. Its hair turned coarse and straggly.

Finally, the white outlines of the forcefield began to return, mercifully enveloping it.

The spindle began to retreat in the direction it had come. As it did so, a burst of mocking laughter sounded, and the saxophonist realized bitterly that he *had* been taken in. After a moment's thought, he brought the mouthpiece of his instrument up to his lips, and began to blow with wild vigour.

NIGHT FLIGHT

Playland became a roaring, inflammatory mass of light and sound, and Deliria looked less and less severe than it had done. Her cold blue light had grown brighter and warmer, as though somewhere an alternative sun was trying to break through. A few colours had even started to appear again in the bleached expanse of her Parkland and Suburbia.

There was still more to be done before the land would be completely released from its tyranny.

Astral Al realized grimly as he flew above it that the only real release it might be able to achieve was total absolution — for no one yet knew what would happen to it, or the things that were in it, after the Transmogrifier had been stopped.

Below his Starstreaker as he sped to the north, he watched the last vestiges of the Golden Gate Park disappearing. There was now no sign of resistance from the Bulls, who had been driven completely away. They retreated into cocoons of their own sound to protect themselves from the live Hawkwind music.

The forces of Deliria's law would return again, however, when the small quantity of fuel in the fairgroundsman's generator had been spent. Then Mankind would be doomed and the victory that the Dark Forces had sought for aeons would truly be won.

He sped on, over the roof-tops of the College of San Francisco, and across an area of large and tightly-grouped semi-detached houses that had once belonged to the comfortable middle-classes. Eventually, these gave way to the thick forests of conifers around the Presidio. In the overgrown landscape appeared the long, squat buildings of the military base, looking uniformly hard and ominous in the weird light. Stretching into the sky behind the base soared the still, colourless towers of the Golden Gate Bridge…a bright orange in the old Earth. The Presidio was intact and, save for the motionless corpses of security guards who had been overpowered by the Hawkwind music, deserted. They lay untidily on the concrete avenues and parade grounds. At sight of them the Starstreaking Hawklord felt a surge of confidence.

A shining, magical aura of light emanated from one of the large Army buildings and he guessed that the Transmogrifier lay inside.

The light was intensely pure and wondrous, and he pondered in amazement how such a radiant thing of beauty could at the same time produce such ugliness.

He felt a bitter irony rise in him at the thought of its destruction, but then he realized that the machines that men put to use for their benefit were in themselves blameless. Like the drug that the drug addict was addicted to, they were pure and innocent.

He brought his Starstreaker down at the steps of the radiant building, and dismounted. The delicate light energy played over his body like a light show. It soothed and caressed him with its paradoxical rays as he withdrew the special Hawkwind tape from its protective casement — the weapon that would be the machine's undoing.

At the foot of the steps lay the toppled bodies of two uniformed Ghouls, their grotesque faces staring sightlessly. Their fleshy protrusions, already decomposing, had burst their suits. The cracks and crevices crawled with tiny parasitic creatures.

Pulling a face at the stench, he ran hurriedly up the steps and burst open the wide double doors.

In front of him lay a vast hall, far greater than the external dimensions of the low building seemed to allow for. It was completely bare, bathed in the soft lights of the Transmogrifier. Its walls and floor shone with a fine opalescence.

The air pulsed with low, rhythmic sounds and he hesitated to enter in case the building was somehow alive and might trap him. But its fragrance and beauty reassured him, and he stepped inside.

A strong feeling of well-being rose inside him. His body felt lighter and less troubled.

Puzzled, he looked around him. The walls were featureless and contained no openings. He wondered where the Transmogrifier was.

The thought occurred to him that the building itself was Transmogrifier, but if this were the case, it did not resemble the machine they had seen in the film sequences shown by the Red Queen.

He lingered in the enchanted light, expecting some inspiration to hit him, but nothing came.

He turned to leave.

As he did so, the hall seemed to shake. He realized without thinking about it that it was crying.

Shocked, he turned back again.

The shaking stopped.

As though out of gratitude, a stairway had materialized in the centre of the hall.

It was a magnificent, decorative staircase fashioned from some kind of precious metal. At the top, it branched into two separate staircases. One climbed to the right and the other climbed to the left, but they seemed to lead nowhere. So far as he could tell from where he stood they ended abruptly in mid air.

He stared at the manifestation uncomprehendingly, his feeling blunted by the waves of pleasure that came off the walls. He realized that the hall wanted him to climb up it.

He set out across the shining floors, and slowly mounted the steps. They were soft under his feet, and the whole staircase swayed and undulated gently as he ascended it.

The hall wanted to please him.

Its wish was an unspoken fact. Its thoughts communed with his own on a level so deep, that he did not realize their meaning until he discovered himself acting them out. They were not harsh orders. They were suggestions he could easily have countermanded had he wanted to do so. So he continued to go along with its wishes, knowing that they would also serve his own.

Now the presentiment of a far stronger need of the hall's came to him. The thoughts troubled his mind, and he found himself worrying for the sake of the hall, yet he didn't know why.

He came to the head of the main staircase, where it split into two. It didn't matter which of the forks he took, so he took the left hand one. As he rounded the corner and looked up he noticed that, from this angle, a room could be seen.

It was a room filled with strange shapes, the tops of which he could see as he mounted the staircase and drew close to its head.

It was a room in the ceiling of a single-story building! His mind boggled.

Cautiously, he extended a booted foot on the floor in front of him.

It was solid.

He walked on it and gazed about him at the objects. They were of all shapes and colours, although only their varied monochrome hues showed that they were, in fact, coloured. They appeared to rest on the floor, or to hover above it, their geometrical surfaces perfectly formed and smooth looking.

In the centre of the shapes towered the Transmogrifier.

It looked like a cathedral with a thousand spires and a central, spherical eye like a doorway. Tall slits like windows showed in its walls, from which fell beams of warm light. The air thumped softly out from it and he knew that inside lay a stupendous force.

The shapes began to move. They rose into the air as though stirred up by an invisible wind. They filled the room, obscuring the Transmogrifier, turning and spinning in the air, never quite touching each other. A powerful, though gentle force seemed to flash between them, preventing them from colliding.

As he watched, the satanic influence of the Death Generator was overpowered, and the shapes began to glimmer with unearthly colours. Their random motion speeded up and he found that they had spread out towards him, and he now stood surrounded by them, charged with the same power of repellence.

The light increased and the shapes burst into full colour, intoxicating him with their intensity. Feelings of destiny washed over him. His Hawk-being radiated with a fresh, new vital force.

With great sorrow he realized that the feeling would have to be short lived. His mind had become inseparably linked with the machine's, and more thoughts had formed inside it. He realized sorrowfully that the machine was going to die.

In his hand he still held the tape, and now he looked at it, and then he looked at the machine's workings and then down at himself.

His sorrow turned to horror as he remembered that it was he who had planned the killing.

Further, that the machine itself wanted to be killed.

I cannot kill you, he finally told the machine.

You must, the Transmogrifier replied. *Or you will destroy your own kind and I will be forced to continue my existence.*

But I thought you and the Red Queen... Astral Al began, confused.

The Red Queen has never owned me. She did not build me. She stole me. Since then I have been forced to serve her wicked mind. But I can no longer bring pain to your kind, and the millions of lifeforms she has hurt and killed along the way.

There must be another way... the Hawklord told it desperately. *I love you. You are so beautiful. Why should you have to die, and she live?*

She will not live, the voice replied. It was warm and caring, and its decision to die out of consideration for their safety brought floods of tears to his eyes. The voice continued soothingly. *Do not upset yourself. You cannot be blamed, and it is not only for you that I wish this. It is for myself, too. There is no way of breaking the programming she has given to me except... with your tape*, it added falteringly. The Hawklord shook with emotion. *Do it now!* The voice spoke more sharply. *Do it before she comes.*

Astral Al looked up. He wiped his eyes. *Where does the tape go?* he asked. *Over here.*

A space formed in the moving, swirling shapes which constituted the inexplicable mind of the Transmogrifier, allowing him to see the cathedral-shaped structure once more. Fighting down his tears he moved towards it. He held the tape at arms' length as though it were unspeakably repugnant to him.

The Power window that flickers, the machine directed him.

Astral Al saw the slit. It flashed rapidly, drawing him towards it. He reached it and held the tape out.

Put it inside, the voice told him. It sounded less controlled now, and a deep panting filled the room. The thudding, omnipresent beat that spread out through the air beat more heavily and irregularly. *Don't worry about me.*

I can't! the Hawklord cried out in mental anguish. "I can't," he screamed. "I can't kill something I love!"

"Then *hate* him!" A cold cruel voice sounded amid the moving shapes.

The Red Queen! the Transmogrifier sighed. *You have been too slow, friend Hawklord...*

The air constricted about him. The swirling shapes began to crash together, the fine balance of the computer's brain upset by the evil emanations of the Red Queen.

Astral Al looked around for her, but she would not show herself.

"You have been foolish beyond words, drummer!" she spat vehemently and with such hatred that the Hawklord physically shrank himself. A sharp pain of anxiety gripped his stomach and he felt like being sick. "I did not know you would come here," she continued. "I did not know you knew where to go..."

"The result of having enemies," Astral Al told her. "You were not hard to trace."

"You will be sorry you came!" she threatened him. "Your music is not so powerful in here, and you are no match for me on your own..."

"Don't come any closer to me!" Astral Al told her savagely.

He decided that he *must do* what he had come to do.

He thrust his hand containing the tape closer to the flashing power window.

Keep it up he spoke mentally to the Transmogrifier. *I'm going to give you the tape.*

A shriek rent the air, so shrill that it took the Hawklord some time to realize from whom it came.

"NO!" the voice screamed in panic. "WAIT!"

It was the Red Queen.

"*Don't* give it the tape..." she spoke hastily. "You don't know what you're doing. If the Transmogrifier is destroyed, Deliria will collapse. We will all die. None of us will win."

"Liar!" Astral Al shouted.

The edge of the tape had entered the power window. The air began to beat wildly again and the shapes moved more freely. "You're always lying. But you won't lie your way out of this one!"

"IT'S TRUE!" she screeched. "Ask the Transmogrifier."

It's true, Al, the Transmogrifier told him.

Stunned, the Hawklord withdrew the tape.

Why didn't you tell me? he asked the Transmogrifier angrily.

There was a guilty silence from the machine.

How long will it take for Deliria to collapse? he asked it.

Not long. You might make it if you hurried back quickly, Al. I meant to tell you but she came...

I don't want to know, Astral Al yelled silently at it.

Impulsively, he stabbed his arm at the shaft of light coming from the power window.

The tape dropped inside, and he turned and fled.

A long piercing scream filled the air.

A crimson stain spread across the room.

Waves of love beat adoringly out at him.

Oh, thanks...Oh, thank you, Al...

Don't thank me, mate.

He ran grief-stricken from the room and down the metal staircase.

Sobs wracked his body.

He ran out across the hall, and ran blindly out into the drab world.

He mounted his Starstreaker and flew off towards the south. There, the crown of light emanating from the live rock band, filled the cavern of night with a million shards of silver.

Freaks with long hair and beads and gaily-coloured hairbands stormed the streets.

Flower Children, armed with Love and idealism and youthful energy sprang, where before had walked hatred, apathy and violence.

These were the improbable products of the Transmogrifier's death throes. Its delicate procreational mechanism had been upset by the Hawkwind tape that had been fed into it.

But the laughter and the merriment of the newly born became the moans and sighs of the dying as their brief life was cruelly ended.

Their disturbing sounds rose and fell in the air as the Hawk drummer fled the deluge.

Deliria was collapsing.

SHEET OF PAIN

Her walls became transparent as she struggled to regain her shape, absorbing immense amounts of heat from the Hawklords' home Time Stream.

Tongues of flame and wreaths of smoke rose from her stricken land as she writhed and twisted in her agony.

The brilliant, golden glow radiating like a sun from the Waltzer, was extinguished. Against the tumultuous wall of dark that replaced it, rose twelve bright balls of light.

The balls hovered hesitantly for a few moments somewhere in front of Astral Al. Then, like elusive UFOs they veered sharply away towards the quaking remains of Haight-Ashbury.

"HEY! WAIT FOR ME!" the Hawklord screamed. "I PUT THE BLOODY TAPE IN!"

Panic stabbed at him.

He felt cheated, effete...storm-tossed as a child, and sped helplessly after the other Hawklords.

He crossed the buckled wreckage of Playland, where the Waltzer's lone light still shone. It illuminated the ghastly shapes of the mutants which, in the sudden absence of the Hawkwind music, had returned briefly to life, crawling and slithering in torment.

In the mêlée he caught a fleeting glimpse of two fearsome figures. They stood where the Hawklords had gigged moments before. One was the golem-like Colonel Goodnight. The other was unidentifiable. He was slender though, and his less heavily-dressed form was partly shrouded in the smoke from the fires.

Something about him fascinated the Hawklord, and momentarily drew him from his course, though delay was dangerous. He flew closer to the figure, and in a deep anguish he realized that he knew who he was — but in its turmoil, his mind could put no name to him.

His ignorance seemed ludicrous and he suffered an agony of indecision, debating whether to go to the hero's aid. But the fascination which had attracted him, now cautioned him, and he hung back, afraid.

The arms of the two giants were raised in conflict, grasping huge swords which they wielded at one another. The pale, enigmatic face of the unknown swordsman was set in a ferocious snarl. It was a mask of such hatred that the Hawklord was certain that the battle was being fought to settle a private vendetta — a score so severe that, to even it, both contestants willingly sacrificed themselves to the flames of Deliria.

Colonel Goodnight, the last servant of the Red Queen, dealt the mysterious hero an unceasing rain of savage, attacking blows — perhaps to defeat an enemy of his Mistress and her crumbling realm.

The hero, for his part, parried defensively against the lethal attacks, sure-footed and fleet. He was less powerful than the other. But his sword was the larger. It was a huge, black monster of a blade, and it seemed to draw on an energy that its bearer looked ill-equipped to give. It slashed and stabbed fiercely at the thick armour of the king mutant, sending showers of silver sparks into the smoky air.

The Hawklord gazed on the spectacle in fear and awe. He watched as the blade turned the tide and became the aggressor, forcing the Colonel on to bended knee. But the mutant fought more determinedly than ever, and they battled on in deadlock — the one never rising from his enforced genuflexion, the other vainly trying to make his opponent's downfall complete.

A kind of berserk frenzy took hold of the hero. He wielded his tireless blade and he cried out a single, rolling word, repeating it with an enraged exasperation.

"Arioch!" he cried. "Arioch!...Help me if you love me!"

The sound of the word rose into the erupting walls of smoke and flame that spurted around them. The sound grew, and it echoed thunderously in the stormy heavens.

A sudden, unknown power made itself felt, and Chaos escalated. A pall of smoke obliterated the battling giants for a moment, and a moan of sadistic pleasure rose from behind the acrid vapours. It was not a human moan. It was a dead, metal susurration that funked the Hawklord to the core.

The smoke cleared and he saw that the black hell blade was aglow with a ghastly opalescence. It now stuck from the eye socket of its helmeted victim. It lingered perversely in its fleshy bed, as the mutant collapsed in an ungainly, ungracious movement to the earth. At length the blade allowed itself to be withdrawn.

The hero turned and cast burning eyes upwards in the direction of Astral Al. His face was bone-white and his hair flowed like a sickly-wax down his neck and on to his shoulders.

But he had not noticed the Hawklord.

He bore a fierce, almost wicked expression of exhilaration, and he flung his arms to the heavens and waved his killer blade triumphantly aloft. He shouted out words that the Hawklord could not understand.

The boiling, sepulchral mass of the Time Zone poured over him. When the smoke cleared the figure of the hero had gone. Where he had stood there was a gaping abyss of fire.

Thick black vapours appeared and as swiftly as the horrific battle scene had appeared, it was lost again in the seething Chaos.

Wracked with grief, the drummer tore himself away from the hateful place. The skull-like face had left an indelible impression on him, though he still did not know why. In the extreme conditions his mind refused to function. He could only see. He could only hear. And he could only feel. And he knew only that he had to tear himself away.

He forced himself to ride high into the exploding sky to escape the erupting ground.

He chased the distant silver balls of light for what seemed like an eternity. They seemed to grow larger, and he thought hopefully that he must be gaining on them. But then they popped out of existence.

His surroundings began to waver and shimmer.

The tops of the tall skyscrapers that still miraculously poked through the smoke bent and shook optically.

The collapsing, desperate world began to fade out of existence.

Blurred and dissolving, the massive, white face of the Ferry Building clock loomed up at him.

He began spiralling helplessly towards it.

Desperately, he tried to regain altitude, but collision was inevitable. He smashed through its shimmering, vaporous surface, deep into the Time Zone wall.

DISTANT SUNS

A grassy field dotted with blue hardbells and white chamomiles materialized around them. It was broken with regular rows of low, gnarled apple trees in full leaf.

The air was filled with the songs of many different birds, sweetly defining their territories, and the hum and call of hidden insects.

Though the sun was shining brightly, the day was strangely chill.

Painfully, the Hawklords picked themselves off the grass. Their bodies were damaged and sore from their ordeal.

"Where are we?" the Thunder Rider asked quietly.

"Dunno," the Boss replied. "Looks like Earth, at least." He rubbed his side, and winced with pain. "Think I've bust a rib."

"It's cold," the Crystal Princess complained. She shivered and stared, entranced, at the paradoxical landscape. "Is it real or are we dreaming?"

Captain Calvert limped over to one of the trees and plucked an apple. He held it up to them. It was shiny and rosy and made them feel hungry. The Captain put it to his mouth and bit deeply into it. He chewed for a while.

"It's real," he said at last. "Tastes all right too." He began munching on the rest of it. After chewing each mouthful and savouring the apple's exquisite flavour, he spat the pieces out. Being a Hawklord, his body was unable to take sustenance in the usual manner.

Gradually the began to notice more of their strange surroundings.

"Look...through the trees," the Laughing God spoke in a voice of wonder.

They followed his lifted arm with their gaze to where a large improbable building stood. It looked like an Aztec temple. It's white stonework seemed new and recently carved. The brilliant coloured murals on its walls seemed freshly painted, and reminded them of the South American sun art they had seen in old museums.

An English apple orchard and an Aztec temple were an incongruous mating, yet here they seemed to blend together perfectly.

On the skyline loomed the Empire State Building.

It stood apart from its usual surroundings, accompanied instead by a patchwork of inextricably mixed landscapes and artifacts.

When they looked more closely they could see that even this work of architecture was incomplete; that its base was, in fact, formed from another building.

Lion, lamb.

Black, white.

Comic, serious.

Hard, soft.

They had mixed, and mixed harmoniously.

"That's it!" the Baron breathed excitedly. He looked happily about him. "You see what's happened. The Displacement Effects..." He seemed happy now, pausing and struggling for the right words. But he had already said enough to make the others aware of the nature of the supreme act of creation which had occurred.

"No Time Zones," the Thunder Rider stated. He looked all around the horizon, grinning. "When Deliria collapsed, she must have taken the rest back with her...where they belong. And good riddance!"

"But this is incredible!" Lord Rudolph said. He ran his hands through the apple leaves. "This was all...a bloody great mess last time we were here."

"Don't question it or it might disappear!" the Sonic Prince told him in good humour.

"Not this time, mate. This is for real!" the bass guitarist declared. He laughed ironically. "To think, mankind's spent his entire existence trying to separate things and keep things apart. Now, ultimately his efforts have come to nothing. You *can* mix people, only you've got to wipe them clean first…"

"Stop bullshitting," Astral Al called out, "and help me up, will you?"

The group of Hawklords looked down at the stricken drummer. He sat on the grass, nursing his bootless foot.

"Something's wrong with it," he complained.

Lord Jefferson bent down and examined his foot.

"What happened to your boots?" he asked.

"Dunno. They didn't make it, I guess. I nearly didn't make it either, you load of…"

"Now, now, boys," the Dealer waved an admonishing finger at them as he noticed their protesting expressions. He looked at Astral Al. "We agreed it would be every man for himself."

The drummer gasped painfully. "I wish I'd just got a bit more of myself, then. Those boots were the best ones I had." He grinned conciliatorily. "But I guess it's better than losing my feet."

He noticed the fairgroundsman who, so far, had remained silent. He grew serious again. "How did you all manage to give Goodnight the slip?"

Thunder Rider swallowed. He seemed, suddenly, to have been put under a great strain, and looked at the drummer with difficulty.

While Astral Al had delivered the tape, Patti and the Children, led by the Boss and the Dealer had successfully broken through into the Time Zone as planned. They had reached the Waltzer in time to help the Hawklords after they had stopped gigging. They had held the Ghouls at bay while the band stowed their gear and tried to make their getaway. But, unhappily, they had failed to break the power of the large mutant chief and his fleet of mounted speakers.

"We couldn't overpower him," the Thunder Rider said at last. "Elric, he…"

"Elric!"

The shock of delayed recognition at last swept over the drummer. Now he realized what event he had witnessed in the doomed Time Zone. A weird feeling suddenly possessed him.

"Elric held them off," the Thunder Rider continued. A sudden depression had fallen on the band, and he looked sadly around him. "I don't think he made it."

The drummer looked mortified. "He didn't," he replied, grating his teeth. He blamed himself bitterly for not intervening and saving the being who had given his life, that they might have their lives.

"He said we should leave him," the Princess spoke hastily. There was pride and respect in her voice. "He said he wanted to help us…and help himself. We didn't want to leave him, but we had no choice. He was the only one who could withstand the Dark Music. He stopped the Colonel and the rest of the cops from operating the mobile speakers…"

As they stood, reliving the drama, their grief was tempered by a cruel sense of relief. It was partly the relief of the living who have experienced the suffering of men who ought by all that was humane, never to have lived, and who had found blissful release in death. And it was the relief of knowing that the legendary swordsman had chosen, finally, to fight on the side of Hawkwind. The Hawklords derived a bitter sense of happiness at the thought that the sorcerer's restless search might at last be at an end, and that his spirit now be at rest.

Low moans and cries began to rise from the bottom of the gently sloping orchard and once more, in the pressing needs of the moment, they forgot their ally from another world.

"The Children!" the Boss shouted in alarm.

He charged off down the hill, clutching his broken rib cage. He was followed by those who were able to keep up with him.

After the children had broken through the Time Zone wall they had ripped off a fleet of the Harley Davidsons to enable them to reach Playland on time. When the Hawklords started leaving on their Starstreakers, they had returned overland the same way, and crashed through in the nick of time.

They and their machines were now sprawled between the numerous objects that made up the montage landscape beyond the orchard. Some had materialized on the roof of a red double-decker bus. Others on the surreal hybridization formed from an ocean liner and the Egyptian Sphinx. Others lay on various bizarre and familiar surfaces, all in great agony and pain.

Some were unconscious and mercifully spared their suffering. But many had revived and were now struggling for their lives in a world still under attack from an increasing level of Death Radiation.

The Generator at Earth's core was giving no respite. Inside Deliria, the Children had been protected by the Hawkwind music. When the music had stopped they had been able, momentarily, to tolerate greatly reduced levels of Radiation as the Time Zone floundered. Now, they had no such protection.

"We must get them back to…" Captain Calvert began, shocked at what he saw. But then he realized that they now, surely, had no preference as to where they made their base. Earth City was truly a state of mind. It was anywhere they cared to make it.

"Fire the Cannons!" he cried instead. "Let's get the remainder of the Human Race up into that temple."

As one, they climbed back on to their machines and they flew to the aid of their long-suffering fans. They flew over the weird and dislocated land…over a land that contained both a promise and a threat.

They shuddered grimly, and each Hawklord and Hawklady knew that they could not rest until the Death Generator was destroyed.

The land would yield no good until the Evil inside it had been eliminated.

They knew too that no man or immortal could become a true Child of The Sun until he or she had learned to live without the necessity of having to impose either Good or Evil…or to have either imposed on them.

THE END OF THE SECOND BOOK OF THE HAWKLORDS

OTHER CREDITS

Music	Hawkwind
Lyrics	Calvert, Moorcock, Brock
Hawkwind Legend	Bob Calvert, Barnie Bubbles, Michael Moorcock
Time Fault Idea & Technical Advice	Geoff Cowie
The Spanish Armada	Radcliffe Town Library
American Advisor	J. Jeff Jones
Mr. Rock 'n Roll	David Britton
Colonel Goodnight and Empty Soup (in "The Time of the Hawklords")	borrowed courtesy of Terry Wilson
Elric	borrowed courtesy of Michael Moorcock
Some Chapter Titles	J.G. Ballard, Ray Bradbury, W.S. Burroughs, Michael Moorcock, The Electric Prunes, Hawkwind, The Doctors of Madness
Ongoing Help	Tony Stimson, Catherine Butterworth, Steve Greenhalgh, Sherry Gold, Christine Butterworth, Doug Smith, Salford Univ. Union Stage Manager, (1975).

Series based on an idea by Michael Moorcock — with special thanks to Piers Dudgeon and Hawkwind personnel, old and new.

UPCOMING RELEASES FROM COLLECTOR'S GUIDE PUBLISHING

SPRING

The Illustrated Book Of Nazareth
By Michael D. Melton
A comprehensive guide to, and in appreciation of Nazareth, the band and their music. Every Nazareth album, from their 1971 self-titled debut to the recent release of *Move Me*, is included in this 172 page guide; numerous rarities, singles, solo material, special releases, and more are also included, documented in over 100 photos.

The Illustrated Collector's Guide To Punk, Part 1 (w/ CD)
By Dave Thompson
Every punk fan will want to have a copy of this detailed guide which includes full listings of bands' line-ups, singles, albums, miscellaneous recordings, career details, cross-references, and a UK chart log, combined with dozens of photos. Packaged in a box set, a corresponding CD is also included.

Led Zeppelin – The Montreux Concerts
This book, a collection of rare live photographs, strikingly documents Led Zeppelin's three legendary visits to Montreux, Switzerland in the early '70s: March 14, 1970, August 7-8, 1971, October 27-28, 1972.

SUMMER

The Illustrated Collector's Guide To Wishbone Ash (w/ CD)
By Andy Powell
Written by Ash guitarist Andy Powell, this extensive book features over 100 photos, with a comprehensive discography of the group, along with complete listings of band line-ups, tours and concert dates, set lists, tour programs and posters, catalogue numbers, videos, songbooks, fanzines, memorabilia, and much more. Also included in the box set is the CD *BBC Radio 1 Live In Concert*, which was originally recorded at the Paris Theatre in 1972.

The Progressive Rock Book, Vol. 1 – North & South American Editon
By Ron Johnston
This incredibly exhaustive book contains complete single and album listings for hundreds of progressive rock bands hailing from North and South America. The listings include LPs, cassettes, CDs, EPs, 45s, bootlegs, imports, and so on.

The Alternative Rock Book
By Alan Cross
A guide to the most important genre of music to emerge in the last fifteen years. This book includes a complete analysis of hundreds of alternative bands, with full listings of albums, singles, band details, etc.

Books For The Music Collector

Available from...
Collector's Guide Publishing Inc

THE HITCHHIKER'S GUIDE TO ELVIS
An A-Z of the Elvis "Universe" by acclaimed author Mick Farren.
ISBN 0-9695736-5-0
$12.95

THE ILLUSTRATED COLLECTOR'S GUIDE TO KATE BUSH
Fully comprehensive discography.
142 pages.
ISBN 0-9695736-0-X
$10.95

THE ILLUSTRATED COLLECTOR'S GUIDE TO HAWKWIND
Available in a box set with "Warrior On The Edge of Time" CD (GN-3931-8).
ISBN 0-9695736-1-8
$28.98

THE ILLUSTRATED COLLECTOR'S GUIDE TO MOTORHEAD
Available in a box set with a new CD compilation, "The Best of Motorhead" (GCD-219-2).
ISBN 0-9695736-2-6
$28.98

OLIVIA: MORE THAN PHYSICAL — A COLLECTOR'S GUIDE
Available in a box set with "Have You Never Been Mellow" CD (GCD-373-2).
ISBN 0-9695736-6-9
$28.98

THE TIME OF THE HAWKLORDS
1976 Michael Butterworth sci-fi novel, available in box set with "Astounding Sounds, Amazing Music" CD (GCD-345-2)
ISBN 1-896522-05-X
$28.98

THE ILLUSTRATED COLLECTOR'S GUIDE TO LED ZEPPELIN
The latest edition of the world's most comprehensive guide to Led Zeppelin.
ISBN 0-9695736-7-7
Paperback $17.95
ISBN 0-9695736-3-4
Hardcover $21.95

Do you have a giant or outrageous record collection? Have you ever considered putting it down on paper? Collector's Guide Publishing Inc. is always looking for writers. Please write us with your ideas at ──▶

To order, send a completed order form (opposite page) and include a check or money order made out to:

COLLECTOR'S GUIDE PUBLISHING INC.
P.O. Box 62034
Burlington, Ontario L7R 4K2   CANADA

COLLECTOR'S GUIDE PUBLISHING ORDER FORM

TITLE	PRICE (U.S.)	QTY.
The Hitchhiker's Guide To Elvis By Mick Farren	$12.95	____
The Illustrated Collector's Guide To Kate Bush By Robert Godwin	$10.95	____
The Illustrated Collector's Guide To Hawkwind By Robert Godwin (w/ *Warriors On The Edge Of Time* CD)	$28.98	____
The Illustrated Collector's Guide To Motorhead By Alan Burridge & Mick Stevenson (w/ *The Best Of Motorhead* CD)	$28.98	____
The Illustrated Collector's Guide To Led Zeppelin paperbk. By Robert Godwin hardcvr.	$17.95 $21.95	____ ____
Olivia: More Than Physical – A Collector's Guide By Gregory Branson-Trent (w/ *Have You Never Been Mellow* CD)	$28.98	____
The Time Of The Hawklords By Michael Butterworth (w/ *Astounding Sounds, Amazing Music* CD)	$28.98	____
Shipping & handling	+ $5.00	
Total	_____	